Corranda's Crown

Written & Illustrated by
Lee Edward Födi

Royal Fireworks Press • Unionville • New York

Royal Fireworks Press
First Avenue, PO Box 399
Unionville, NY 10988-0399
TEL: (845) 726-4444
FAX: (845) 726-3824
email: rfpress@frontiernet.net

ISBN: 0-88092-573-6

Printed in the United States of America on acid-free, recycled paper
using soy-based inks by the Royal Fireworks Printing Company
of Unionville, New York.

Visit the author's website at www.leefodi.com

LIST OF CHAPTERS

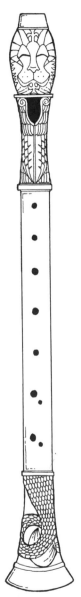

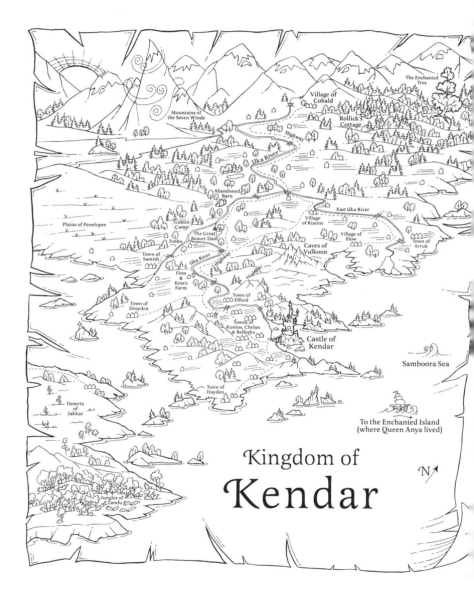

The Enchanted Tree

Village of Cobald

Rollick's Cottage

Mountains of the Seven Winds

Highway

Uka River

Abandoned Barn

East Uka River

Plains of Penelopee

Goblin Camp

Village of Rianne

Embo

The Great Beaver Dam

Village of Illow

Town of Arruk

Caves of Vulkoon

Town of Samish

Uka River

Highway

Finn & Kess's Farm

Town of Elford

Town of Droyden

Towns of Kontos, Chelan & Belforks

Castle of Kendar

Samboora Sea

Town of Hayden

Deserts of Jakkar

To the Enchanted Island
(where Queen Anya lived)

Kingdom of
Kendar

N

Jungles of Zamfu

Chapter 1

✵

A Land Besieged

Dark times had fallen upon the kingdom of Kendar. The entire land was overrun with goblins, a strange and hideous breed of creatures that were threatening to cripple the very livelihood of the nation. Across the land, scholars, academics, and Kendar's most learned citizens pondered and debated the mysterious origin of the goblins, but not even the most scientific minds could explain their appearance, nor produce a solution for ending the infestation. Slippery and sneaky, the goblins preferred the darkness of night, and they were near impossible to catch. Those that were caught seemed to be replaced by new goblins almost immediately. The situation seemed hopeless. Only one thing was for certain: the goblins were multiplying with each passing day, while Kendar's human population seemed to be slowly disappearing, one by one.

The goblins themselves were repugnant monsters. They had greasy gray flesh and scraggly, misshapen bodies covered with warts. Their eyes were large and round, while their noses were either large and fleshy or long and hooked, bubbling with pimples and sprouting curly hairs. Some had ears so long and twisted that no cap or hood would cover their heads, while others sported jagged, rotting teeth caked

1

with the leftovers of last week's meals. They did not walk, but rather skittered or crawled, sometimes on all fours, moving about on disfigured limbs that creaked and clicked with bony joints. Even their names were ugly, for the goblins were called such vulgar things as Kanker or Tick, or maybe Flem or Fester; still others went by the likes of Retch and Rott and Skab and Skurvy.

Some of the beasts were tall and lean, while others were fat and squat with huge bellies that burst the buttons on their clothes—if they were to wear any, which many did not. They came in many shapes and sizes, though it was hard to say if any was more repulsive than the next or the last. Still, despite their varied appearances, the goblins shared one common trait: their cruel, crooked hearts. Indeed, it was as if someone had stolen all the best parts of human nature, only to leave behind that which was greedy and grotesque.

As the years passed and the goblins continued to increase in number, it became obvious that the vile vermin were being controlled by a single source of dark magic. Many rumors spread across the land, but most people believed that the person behind the goblin plague was the strange and secretive witch known as Odjin the Beautiful. The sorceress was well named, for she was as enchanting and becoming as the goblins were ugly. In truth, there was only one thing more important to Odjin than her beauty, and that was power. She hungered for power as a tempest hungers to rain upon the earth, and she made it no secret that she had desires for the throne of Kendar.

At last, the goblin infestation grew to such epidemic

proportions that Kendar's King Daron and Queen Anya called Odjin before their court to plead for the witch's aid. Odjin was no stranger to the palace. She had grown up in the castle and in her youth had been a good friend to King Daron. Odjin's fascination with black magic, however, had slowly created a rift between the two and by the time Daron took the throne as Kendar's king, he and the sorceress were barely on speaking terms. Now they were true enemies and it was only in this grave crises that King Daron would even tolerate Odjin's presence in his castle.

As the sorceress was ushered into the palace, the guards and courtiers gasped at her stunning beauty. Odjin was tall, slender, and pale, with long golden hair that fell upon her shoulders in a cascade of thick curls. Her eyes were blue with long fluttering lashes and her lips were round and full. She carried a golden mirror with a long curving handle that she used to gaze vainly upon her reflection throughout the day. She was proud and confident in her beauty, and she wielded it like a weapon.

Odjin made no secret of her hostile nature as she entered the royal throne room. She refused to kneel or even curtsy before the king and queen. Daron scowled at the witch, while Anya's kitten rose from the queen's lap to arch her back with a threatening hiss.

"Easy, Pasha," Queen Anya whispered in a soothing voice, gently stroking her pet. "You must display better manners than this for our guest."

"Horrid creatures," Odjin remarked as she paused to stare at her reflection in her long-handled mirror. "I, for one, cannot abide animals."

"Yet you abide these horrific goblins," King Daron said. "These beasts have nearly taken over our entire land! They consume our crops and sully our rivers. Soon there will be nothing left of Kendar!"

"Your appraisal of the situation is certainly dramatic, if nothing else," Odjin said.

"You think I overstate the seriousness of this matter?" Daron demanded.

"No, it is a dreadful plight," Odjin said with a slight curl of her lips. "Yet I fail to see what any of this has to do with me!"

"Let us dispense with these games," King Daron snapped. "For all I know, these aberrations of nature are

5

being churned from the spells of your very own cauldron. But if you have not made the goblins, Odjin, then at the very least I believe you control them."

"Really, my lord," Odjin mocked, coiling a strand of her hair about one finger, "you grant me far too much credit."

"I grant you nothing," King Daron growled, slamming his fist on the arm of his throne so hard that the lords and ladies of the court winced at his passionate anger. "But I know that you want something. It's your way. So tell me what it is, Odjin. Tell me what it will take for you to end this madness."

Odjin looked up from behind her golden locks, and smiled sadly. "Alas, my Lord," she murmured, "you, of all people, should know what I desire."

"That which you know you cannot have," King Daron retorted.

"Odjin, this behavior does not become you," Anya interrupted. "Let us negotiate an end to this situation in good faith."

"Yes," King Daron agreed. "Name your price, Odjin, to end this plague!"

"My price!?" Odjin hissed, "My price!? Wealth, power, domination!" The witch paused to laugh, and the court stirred nervously at her erratic behavior. "But I know you shall give me none of these things," Odjin added. "So then I will ask for one thing, my king, one thing only."

"Then name it," King Daron said, his voice growing uneasy.

"Look into my eyes, my lord," Odjin pleaded. "Gaze deep

into my eyes and know my beauty."

"No!" King Daron cried, and he instantly cast his eyes away. "It's a trick! No one look into this witch's eyes, lest you fall under her power! Curse you, Odjin! I don't know what plots you are hatching, but I will not have you casting your spells in my court!"

"Fool!" Odjin sneered. "You've had your chance, Daron. The next time we meet, I shall not be so civil."

"Be gone with you, Odjin," King Daron proclaimed, rising out of his throne to stand at his full height. Despite his age, he was still an intimidating figure, and even Odjin flinched as he spoke his next words. "You have defied me once too often and now your insidious nature has been betrayed here, for all to see. So if you will not help Kendar, then as far as I'm concerned, you're against it. So be gone with you! If I could prove that you were behind this plague, then I would cast you in irons! But our laws are just and true, and without this proof you must go free."

Odjin locked her eyes upon the king, and though he would not directly return her stare, Daron could feel the hatred that flowed from her heart. "Very well," the witch finally said. With a flick of her hair, she turned her back on Kendar's throne and left the court with a strong, deliberate gait.

Queen Anya's kitten watched the witch go with a parting snarl.

"Yes, Pasha," Queen Anya whispered, as she scratched the kitten's gray ears. "I sense it as well. She harbors a dangerous power beneath her beauty."

King Daron dismissed the courtiers and with a heavy sigh sunk wearily into his throne. As a young man Daron had been a man of valor and courage, but now he was old and weary, his once fire-red hair turned gray like the ash of a barren hearth.

"This is my fault," King Daron fretted to his wife, now that the court was empty and they were left in private. "Odjin's anger against Kendar begins with me, and yet now I am too old to fight her, while she remains young and strong."

"You must have faith, Daron," Anya told him. "You do not fight this battle alone."

"Aye," the King murmured sadly. "But the kingdom seems to have aged with me. We have become nothing more than a court of old, complacent men."

"You do Kendar much discredit," Anya claimed. "Do

not underestimate our strength."

"A kingdom's strength begins with its leader," Daron stated. "Once I was strong, but now I have failed Kendar. I have not even left an heir to lead her into the future, no prince to defend her."

"No, not yet," Anya said.

"Not yet? What do you mean, not yet?" Daron asked. "We have tried to have children for twenty years, all without hope. Now it's too late."

"It's never too late," Anya said, taking Daron's hand and comforting him with her warm brown eyes.

"Your optimism never ceases to amaze me," Daron confided to his queen. "An heir? How do you think we will manage it now, so late in our lives?"

"Because I am with child now, Daron," Anya whispered, leaning over to kiss her husband on the cheek. "You will be a father yet!"

"A father!?" Daron exclaimed, his eyes opening wide with astonishment. Anya let out a girlish laugh at Daron's reaction. In spite of himself, the king's face was now beaming with happiness, melting the grimace that had consumed his features only moments before.

"It's good to see I can make you smile yet," Anya told him.

"Me, a father? At my age?" Daron murmured in disbelief.

"You see, there are miracles at work within the world yet," Anya told her husband, caressing his arm. "Dark times may lie ahead, but still there is hope."

Chapter 2

ꙮ

The Army of Darkness

Upon leaving King Daron's court, Odjin immediately returned to her secret lair, deep in the cavernous mountains of Vulkoon. The mountains were tall and foreboding, with craggy black cliffs and sharp peaks. Green meadows and forests had once covered the mountain range, but now nothing lived there at all, unless you counted Odjin and her swarm of insatiable goblins.

It was here, in the dark and sinister labyrinth of caves, that Odjin practiced her black arts and plotted against the kingdom of Kendar. Through the years, the sorceress had bided her time with patience and cunning, while slowly building her goblin army. Now, with her hordes swelling into a force so immense that its numbers could not be easily counted, Odjin knew there would be no better time than the present to attack Kendar and seize power once and for all.

With this in mind, Odjin summoned before her the leader of her goblin army, a particularly disgusting creature known as Captain Wort. The repulsive goblin was so fat that his belly sagged well over his trousers, threatening to snap his belt with the merest belch. His obese frame was supported by two scrawny legs, while his arms were so long that his hands dragged the ground when he stooped. He had

but five jagged teeth in his entire head, and these were so rotted with cavities that they had long ago turned yellow and brown.

Odjin watched her vulgar servant lurch into the room and greeted him with gnashing teeth.

"I see once again you have neglected to bathe," Odjin retorted. "How many times have I warned you not to come before me emitting such a sour stench?"

"Me sorry, oh great witchy," Wort mumbled. "Me forget to washy."

"Never mind that now," Odjin said with a wave of her hand. "I have been at the court of King Daron. He and his pesky queen have begged me to call off you and your blemished brethren, Wort!"

"You do it, Mistress?" Wort asked, kneeling before the beautiful sorceress. "Listen to kingy?"

"Never!" Odjin cried. "Daron is quaking in his boots at the thought of a few goblins destroying a farm here and there! Ha! This is nothing compared to what awaits him!"

Wort giggled with glee at the witch's threat. "What we do next?" the goblin asked, scratching his large, wart-infested chin.

"Prepare your army," Odjin ordered, turning to look at herself in her mirror. "Tomorrow we shall lay waste to the countryside. We shall stop for nothing. Not until we take the castle of Kendar itself!"

"Castle?" Wort cried. "We dares!?"

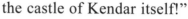

"Of course we dare!" Odjin snapped. "Kendar has suffered under Daron's rule for long enough! I shall be the new queen and the people will know my power!"

Captain Wort was now dancing about the cavern on his long, uneven legs, unable to restrain his giddiness. "Yes, yes, mistress! We ruley whole land!"

Odjin turned suddenly from her mirror. "We?" she asked venomously.

"Well—er, me means you, of course, oh mistress!" Wort stuttered.

"Yes, and don't you forget it, my dear, incompetent buffoon," Odjin hissed. "You and your pungent, scab-ridden, pestilence-spreading breed are here to serve me! Without me, you would not even exist!"

"Yes, yes," Wort whimpered, scurrying quickly away into the shadows.

Odjin turned back to admire her reflection and ran her fingers through her long golden hair. "Yes," she murmured softly to herself. "Everything has transpired according to my plan! Kendar will soon be mine!"

The next morning the witch stood at the edge of the caves of Vulkoon and looked down upon her goblin throng. Her mere presence was enough to stir them into hysterics. Armed with clubs, axes, and all weapons of horror, the savage goblins could barely contain their desire for battle.

Odjin raised her pale arms to the sky and spoke in a bone-chilling voice. "For years I have promised you this great day," the witch proclaimed. "At last, our time has come. All of Kendar shall shudder at our coming! So go forth, my vile vassals, and make war!"

And with these words the witch unleashed her army of darkness upon the land in an attack so horrific it was like the bursting of a volcano. Voracious and frenzied, the goblins swept through the land in a tidal wave of devastation, rav-ishing and plundering all that stood in their path.

Chapter 3

❧

Guardians of the Crown

K endar was not well prepared for the goblin attack. For twenty years the kingdom had known only peace and King Daron's soldiers were without experience or proper training. They fought valiantly against the invading goblins, yet battle after battle saw the defeat of Kendar's army. And while King Daron's army shrank with each loss, the goblin ranks seemed to grow only larger and stronger. As the war raged deep into the winter months, Kendar's forces were pushed steadily back towards their last outpost—the castle itself.

Despite the fact that her country was mired in war, Anya was proceeding smoothly in her pregnancy. The queen was of good health and spirit, and the entire country seemed to be waiting with bated breath for the birth of the royal child.

Then, one stormy winter night, a royal messenger came charging into King Daron's camp near the front lines of the battlefield.

"My lord, I bring news," the messenger panted. "Queen Anya is in labor—I expect she shall give birth before the morn comes!"

"Bring me a fresh horse!" King Daron called to his servants as he threw on his heavy riding cloak. "With any luck

I will make the castle by dawn!"

Daron rode through the dark night, over the icy fields and beneath the forest boughs that bent and twisted over the road with the weight of the winter snows. By the time he arrived at the gates of the castle, tiny icicles clung to his beard and his cloak was white with frost. Still, nothing could stop the weary king from going immediately to his wife in the royal bed chamber. Here he found her in a deep slumber, cradling within her arms a child so small and delicate that Daron felt his heart leap at the sight of such a beautiful thing.

Daron approached the bed and gazed with happiness upon his wife and child. After a few moments, Anya awoke and saw her husband.

"Daron," she whispered happily. "Meet your daughter."

She handed the child to Daron and the king felt his daughter tremble with life as he held her for the first time. He felt she must be the most miraculous thing he had ever beheld. Her hair was red like autumn leaves, and she kicked with strength and vitality.

"She is lively for such a tiny thing," Daron remarked.

"Yes," Anya agreed with a content nod. "She courses with the blood and passion of Kendar!"

"We have not even decided upon a name yet," Daron reminded his wife. "Have you any thoughts, Anya?"

"Yes," the queen replied. "I want to call her Corranda, for this is a name from my own country. It is a powerful name and means 'One-Who-Walks-With-The-Earth'."

"Then Corranda it shall be," Daron agreed. "Let the news go across the kingdom! Kendar has its heir!"

The birth of Princess Corranda gave the people of Kendar a glimmer of hope amidst the dark times of the goblin war. King Daron and Queen Anya had tried their entire marriage to have a child; now that they had finally succeeded, the people took it as a sign that better times were ahead. As heir to the throne, Corranda would one day be Kendar's queen and the people hoped she would have the strength to deliver them from their enemies.

Corranda, of course, would need to grow up before she could accomplish any such purpose and the immediate threat of the goblin invasion was too pressing to await her adulthood. Indeed, by the time Corranda was only three months old, the

witch's troops had crushed the last of Kendar's army, forcing King Daron and his few remaining men to retreat to the royal castle of Kendar.

The castle was situated on a rocky island in the middle of the Uka River, connected to the bank by only a single bridge. Because of this, the castle had always been easy to defend, and throughout the centuries had outlasted many sieges. Odjin's army, however, was unlike any other, and the goblins overcame the great river moat with ease. Armed with torches, catapults, and battering rams, the horrendous beasts soon sat poised at the very gates of the castle.

Alas, the king and queen knew the kingdom was on the verge of defeat and they called forth their two most trusted advisors, Rollick the Dwarf and Belarus the Brave.

Rollick and Belarus were good friends, though in truth they made an odd pair. Belarus was as tall as Rollick was short and had to bend nearly double just to hear the dwarf speak. Belarus himself talked very little. He preferred to lead by example, rather than words. He was the most respected knight in King Daron's court, a stature earned by years of service to the throne. In his prime, Belarus had been a great warrior and had fought many campaigns at King Daron's side. The knight still displayed great skill on the battlefield, though now his face was lined with deep wrinkles and his hair had turned gray to match the color of his eyes.

Unlike Belarus, Rollick was a talkative man who was ever willing to engage in some argument or debate. The dwarf's eyes were keen and sharp, complemented by a pair of shaggy eyebrows and a furled brow that betrayed his serious mind. He had a large round nose and a thick bushy beard that he kept trim and neat with a small silver comb. Rollick was a brave man, and through the years had never shied from his duty, regardless of its dangers. Indeed, people often remarked that Rollick's courage could not be measured by his size.

"Welcome, my friends," King Daron said as Rollick and Belarus came before him and Anya in their private tower.

"How may we serve you?" Rollick asked anxiously.

"Defeat is ours," Daron replied sternly. "Even as we speak, Odjin hurls her forces against the castle and these walls will soon crumble before her might."

"We will fight to the end," Belarus vowed.

"No," Daron said. "Your time for fighting has passed. Now you will turn your minds to a more important task."

Rollick and Belarus exchanged a quizzical glance, unsure of the meaning behind the king's strange words.

"The princess," Queen Anya explained. "You must take Corranda from here so that she may be spared the witch's fury."

"We will do everything in our power to protect the princess," Belarus promised, never one to question his orders.

Rollick, on the other hand, had objections, and voiced them immediately. "I don't like the sound of this," the dwarf declared. "Surely you will escape with us?"

"Nay," replied Anya, as she cradled the princess in her arms. "Our place is with the people of Kendar, and we will not abandon them in this tragic hour."

"I strongly advise against this course of action," Rollick protested. "Leave Belarus and I behind to deal with Odjin.

You escape with Corranda—it's best to keep your family together and safe."

"Where would we hide?" Queen Anya asked. "We cannot disguise ourselves. Our faces are on every coin—we are known throughout the land! The key to Corranda's safety is secrecy!"

"Leave Kendar!" Rollick urged. "We'll smuggle you to another country where you will be safe! You can return to your own land, Queen Anya, your native country."

"Kendar is my home now," Queen Anya said firmly. "How could I live with myself, safe and secure, while the country I have come to love is enslaved?"

"The decision is final," King Daron said with a heavy voice. "We will stay with the people and share their fate."

He placed his hands upon the small man's shoulders. "It will be all right, my old friend," he told the dwarf. "Your emotions serve you well, but now you must focus on the matter at hand. The princess. You must think of her now."

"Guard her well," Queen Anya said. "It will one day be her duty to take her rightful position on the throne."

Rollick pulled a handkerchief from his pocket to wipe the tears from his eyes, and even Belarus cleared his throat uncomfortably as he tried to choke back his sadness.

"Very well," Rollick murmured reluctantly. "I will do as you wish."

"We have prepared provisions for your journey," Anya told the two men, gesturing to some packs that lay near the tower door. "You will find clothes and food, as well as some milk for Corranda."

"My queen, I know nothing of looking after a baby!" Rollick admitted, suddenly realizing the predicament that lay before him.

"You will have to learn," Daron stated. "These packs contain some jewels and coins as well, though you must be careful how you spend them. Kendar is a poor country now, its coffers drained by this war. Any extravagant purchases may draw suspicion."

"My lord," Belarus spoke up, "where shall we go?"

"This I cannot tell you," Daron replied. "Nor do I want to know. Odjin's powers are immense—she may be employing her dark magic to listen to this very conversation! No, it is better this way. Decide between yourselves where you shall go, and tell no one."

"There is one more thing I would ask of you," Anya

added. "As you have said, Rollick, I am not from this land. My people are not so different from those of Kendar. Still we have customs and traditions that are very important to me. I ask you to raise Corranda with these traditions. Teach her to know nature, to live in harmony with it. My people do not harm animals for any reason; we are not meat eaters. I ask that you raise Corranda to be the same."

"I promise that your daughter shall know the spirit of your people," Rollick declared.

Queen Anya nodded solemnly, then turned her attention to Corranda for the last time. She gently kissed the child on the back of the neck, and by this act left the mark of a crown upon her daughter, for the queen was not without her own small magic. Rollick and Belarus gasped with amaze-

ment. They had always known Anya possessed special abilities, but had never seen her demonstrate such magic.

King Daron himself was not surprised by Anya's enchantment. He took his daughter and held her before his tearful eyes. "Now you are forever sealed with the sign of royalty, Corranda," he decreed. "No one shall ever be able to challenge your right to the throne."

"Now go," Anya ordered Rollick and Belarus as the king handed Corranda over to the two men. "Time grows short!"

"May strength and courage go with you," Daron said.

With these final words, King Daron and Queen Anya sent the two men on their way with the Princess Corranda. They never saw their daughter again, for Daron and Anya perished in that tower, defending their kingdom to the last from Odjin's dark army. They died together, and with peace, for they knew Corranda was safe in the guardianship of the tall, quiet knight and the wise old dwarf.

Chapter 4

જી

Escape and Capture

Rollick and Belarus fled with the princess down the twisting tunnels and spiraling stairwells of the castle. Corranda struggled and sobbed within Rollick's strong arms, but he held her close to his chest, doing his best to soothe her.

In the bottom of the castle there was a secret passage which was known only to the king, the queen, and Corranda's two guardians. This secret tunnel burrowed underneath the Uka River and led into the forests on the far bank of the delta. Rollick knew that their escape would be assured so long as they could reach the passage.

The two companions were still far from the hidden tunnel, however, when they suddenly heard a tremendous crash which caused the castle to tremble from its highest towers to its very foundations.

"What on earth was that?!" Rollick exclaimed.

"The castle gates," Belarus answered sadly. "They have been breached by the goblin horde!"

"Quickly!" Rollick urged. "We must make even greater haste!"

In only a matter of minutes, dozens of goblins were in hot pursuit of Rollick and Belarus, chasing the two brave

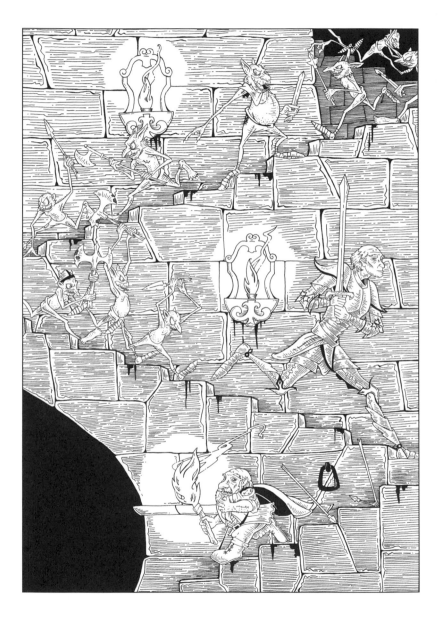

24

heroes through the cavernous depths of the castle.

"We shall be overtaken!" Rollick gasped.

"This will not do!" Belarus shouted from behind Rollick. "One must fall to save the rest!"

"No!" Rollick cried, turning quickly to confront his friend. "We must stay together!"

"It's the only way!" Belarus argued. He lifted his great sword and turned to face their pursuers. "Go to the tunnel and save Corranda!"

Rollick saw that Belarus had already made up his mind. Even as Rollick fled down the stairs, he heard the clash of his friend's sword as the noble knight turned to meet the onslaught of goblin attackers.

Belarus fought with passion and courage, and though his foes were many, he did not allow a single goblin to squeeze past him.

Rollick finally reached the secret passage, deep in the dark belly of the castle. The noise of the goblin invasion was now nothing more than a faint din. Still, the dwarf looked about him carefully to ensure that he was not being watched. Once he was certain he and Corranda were alone, Rollick pressed his hand against a small lever in the floor and a section of the wall rolled slowly back to reveal the hidden passage. With only a single torch to guide him, Rollick disappeared into the blackness of the tunnel, and the door closed behind him to disguise his escape route.

When he reached the safety of the forest on the other side of the river, Rollick paused to catch his breath and look upon the surrendered castle of Kendar. Many of the palace towers were engulfed in flames, with great pillars of

black smoke bellowing forth from their spires.

"Alas," Rollick murmured sadly to the infant Corranda, "I fear you will never see your father and mother again."

In the meantime, Belarus the Brave was defeated in his virtuous battle against the goblins. Captain Wort brought the knight in shackles before Odjin on the ruined grounds of the castle.

"Look upon your new queen," Odjin hissed as Belarus was forced to kneel before her. "I have conquered Kendar and defeated your king and queen. Your loyalty now belongs to me, fair knight, so tell me at once where the princess babe has been taken."

"No I shall not," Belarus declared boldly. He was exhausted and covered with dirt and the wounds of battle, but he was determined to challenge the witch's beauty.

"Poor, brave fool," Odjin laughed haughtily. "No one can resist me."

She looked upon him, but Belarus immediately cast his eyes to the ground.

"Dare not look away from me!" Odjin commanded angrily. She grabbed Belarus by the chin and forced him to stare upon her face. "Gaze into my eyes, brave soldier, and know my power!"

Belarus squirmed to break free, only to feel the sharp jab of Captain Wort's sword in the back of his neck.

No longer could Belarus resist. He looked deep into Odjin's glassy eyes and gasped as he was confronted with her strong, voluptuous beauty. At that moment, he was so overcome with pangs of desire for Odjin's love that he instantly began to transform into something strange and grotesque. His once mighty muscles shriveled to the bone and his noble jaw began to sprout warts and long black hairs. His eyes became giant and yellow, while his skin became gray and spotted. He had transformed into a beast so repulsive that to look at him was not even to recognize the slightest glimmer of the man he had once been. Alas, Odjin had stolen from him everything he had: his strength, his courage, his very soul. Such was the fate of anyone who was enchanted by the witch's unspeakable beauty, for Odjin was not capable of giving love, but only consuming it, and she drained it from her victims' hearts until they were left empty, deformed, and ugly.

"Your name is Belarus no more," Odjin declared as she stood over the cowering goblin. "Now you shall be known as Callus, and my every whim shall be your command."

"Yes, yes!" Belarus whimpered in his new, misshapen state. "Me lovey you, Odjin! Me does your wishes!"

"Of course you do," the witch said. "I demand of you: where is the princess?"

"Mistress," Callus drooled, "princess escapes with ugly little dwarfy! Once dwarfy my friendy friend. Now me hates him, ugly little dwarfy!"

"Yes, yes, I understand," Odjin said coolly. "I appreciate your loyalty, my scraggly little Callus! But tell me about the princess!"

"Little baby has crown on neck," Callus explained. "Little marky mark. So you knows it when you finds true princess."

"Excellent," Odjin chortled, turning to Captain Wort. "Today is a great day, Worty. It has not only seen the end of Daron, but it shall see the end of his line! Search the entire land, Wort! Ransack every village and every farm! Leave no stone unturned!"

"Yes!" Wort lisped. "Me catches little baby for Odjin!"

Callus revealed to Odjin the existence of the secret passage in the castle of Kendar and Wort and his soldiers tracked Rollick through the tunnel and into the woods.

Once they reached the forest, however, they discovered that Rollick had been careful to cover his tracks and they had no idea as to the dwarf's direction. Wort scoured the kingdom in search of the missing princess and yet, after several weeks, he could find no trace of her.

Throughout Kendar, the hope that had first emerged when Corranda was born now flourished into an unfettered faith that the princess would one day return to conquer Odjin the Beautiful. Of course, when Odjin heard these stories the rage boiled inside her like the rumbling of a thunderstorm and she vowed never to relent in her search for the girl marked by the symbol of a crown.

"She just wee little baby," Wort told Odjin. "Little baby not hurt Odjin! Why so afraids of her?"

"I'm not afraid of her, you scurrilous, scat-feeding slave!" Odjin retorted, hurling a nearby vase at the head of the hapless goblin. "Don't you see? The princess herself is not dangerous—it's the hope she represents to the people! Crush the hope and you crush the spirit of the people!"

"Oh," Wort murmured. "You wants me crushy little wee princess?"

"No, you fool!" Odjin yelled angrily. "You can't crush her until you find her! Just find her! Find me that wretched child!"

With that Wort scampered away, before the witch could fling something heavier than a vase. Odjin watched the pitiful creature skitter into the shadows, then turned to brood upon her icy reflection, her mind soured with thoughts of the missing princess.

Chapter 5

❧

A Kingdom in the Forest

ollick knew all too well that Odjin would be obsessed with finding Princess Corranda. He realized that he would not only have to hide the princess well, but for a long, long time.

As he camped out that first night of their escape and fed Corranda on the goat's milk Queen Anya had provided, Rollick remembered a tiny village he had once visited in the far northern reaches of Kendar. The village was called Cobald and was surrounded by a vast wilderness that would serve well to hide Rollick and Corranda from Odjin's hunting parties. The more Rollick thought about the place, the more he liked it.

His mind was soon made up and the dwarf turned north with his tiny ward. The way was not easy and Rollick had many near encounters with the goblins who were busily combing the countryside for the missing princess. By keeping off the main roads, Rollick managed to avoid trouble, and after several weeks he reached the quiet mountain vale of Cobald.

Rollick immediately knew he had made the right decision. Cobald was in such a remote part of Kendar that Odjin's rule was not so harshly felt. The land was still lush and green, for the goblins had not yet migrated so far north in their quest to indulge their insatiable appetite for food and destruction. Even so, Rollick did not linger long in the village, leaving its relative comforts behind for the seclusion of the nearby forest. Here, in a small cottage deep in the mountain woods, Rollick set up his new life, living under the guise of a lonely woodsman raising his orphaned niece.

The dwarf confided in no one about his secret, though in truth, he and Corranda came in contact with few people. Cobald was a good day's ride from the cottage, and Rollick rarely took Corranda into the village unless he was in need of some tool or provision.

Rollick and Corranda lived a quite, humble life in the forest. The dwarf was a handy carpenter and most of the possessions they owned he built or carved with his own two hands. This included not only the cottage, but most of the furniture in it, and even a stable for their milk cow Jumba, who Rollick had purchased in Cobald with a few of the coins entrusted to him by Queen Anya and King Daron.

Rollick had built the cottage in a tiny glade in the woods where the trees were sparse enough to allow the sun to beam upon their doorstep. A small gurgling brook ran near the cottage. Water was plentiful and Rollick planted a little garden to grow peas, onions, carrots, grain, and beans. When she grew old enough, Corranda helped Rollick pick berries and wild mushrooms and together they made pies and delicious vegetable stews. Jumba provided them with milk, cheese, and butter, and sometimes eggs were to be had from the nests of quail or wild ducks.

It was a simple life, unlike Rollick had ever known. Gone were the days of fine living in the palace of Kendar, with its extravagant banquets and festivals. The old dwarf's beard grew long and gray and he no longer had a tiny silver comb with which to groom it. His hands crew calluses and his joints would ache as he spent his days in physical labor rather than in playing chess with Belarus or planning strategy with King Daron.

Yes, his friends were gone, but the dwarf realized that he had gained something far greater in exchange for his old life: a family. Rollick had never had children of his own and the aging man came to cherish Corranda's companionship and love. To his astonishment, Rollick was happier than he had ever been, and he could not help thinking that he and Corranda had created their own private kingdom deep in the mountainous forest of Kendar, a kingdom so secret that only he and the princess even knew it existed.

As Corranda grew older she began to ask about her parents, but Rollick decided to hide the truth from her, too.

"Your parents died when you were just a baby," Rollick told Corranda as a child. "Your father was a blacksmith and your mother a seamstress. We lived in the southern part of Kendar in those days; but then the goblins came, bringing disease and famine to the land. Your parents became sick and after they passed away, I decided to take you and go north, far away from the goblins as possible."

Rollick did not like to lie to the girl, but he was reluctant to burden her with the knowledge of her royal heritage until she was old enough to understand it. He called her by the simple name of Corra and ensured that she kept her hair

34

long and unruly so as to conceal the mark of the crown, a mark which Corranda herself was not even aware that she possessed.

Rollick fulfilled the wishes of Queen Anya, raising the princess to love nature. He trained Corranda to survive in the woods, showing her which plants and roots were edible and those which had healing powers. He taught her to respect and value the forest, and to share it with the birds and animals that lived there.

In time Corranda came to develop a close relationship with the forest creatures, treating them with a kind, almost motherly affection. If she found a baby bird fallen from its nest, she would gently return it to its home; or if she came upon a wounded rabbit, she would nurse it back to health, then set it free in the wild.

"You have great talent with these creatures," Rollick remarked one afternoon as he watched Corranda help an orphaned fawn learn to walk. "It reminds me of your mother, for she too had a very close connection with the animal kingdom."

"Really?" Corranda asked. "What kind of connection?"

"It seemed to me that she could almost speak with animals," Rollick explained, stroking his beard with his stubby fingers. "I asked her about it once, but she just smiled at me as if it was a secret she was not willing to tell."

"I wish I had known her," Corranda said.

"She was a beautiful person," Rollick said. "And she would be very proud of you, Corra."

Corranda sighed. This was her greatest sorrow in life, that she had never known her real parents. As she grew older, Corranda had found herself wanting to know everything she could about her family, but Rollick would tell her very little. The old dwarf was a kind and gentle provider, but he could never completely replace her need for her parents, especially the companionship of a mother.

"Is everything all right, Corra?" Rollick asked, placing his hand on the girl's shoulder while she watched the little fawn wobble across the grass on untried legs.

"Yes, uncle," Corranda replied.

She looked into the dwarf's warm eyes and remembered to count her blessings, too. She loved her uncle and was grateful for the wisdom and affection he showed her each and every day.

By the age of fifteen, Corranda had blossomed into a thoughtful young woman. She had lively, brown eyes and her hair was still as red as the day she was born. She wrote poetry and played music, yet she could also work just as hard as Rollick, and often did.

She did not look like a princess, for she had no fine gowns or jewelry to grace her simple beauty. She appeared no more than a peasant girl, but even so, Rollick could see that Corranda resonated with the qualities of her parents, the qualities of a leader.

It was a bittersweet happiness for the old dwarf. He knew Corranda would make a great queen, yet his heart ached at the thought of sending her out in the world to confront the evil witch, Odjin the Beautiful.

Chapter 6

❧

The Enchanted Tree

The summer that Corranda turned fifteen, Rollick made plans to take her on a camping trip. Corranda hoped her uncle would take her to the village of Cobald or further south to one of the larger towns, for she had a yearning to see more of the country. After all, she already lived in the woods and, in her opinion, camping was no grand adventure.

"It's safer this way," Rollick justified; it was the excuse he used whenever Corranda expressed her desire to leave the forest. "Kendar is a dangerous country to travel, what with all the goblins about. Every year there seem to be more and more of them."

"But I've never even seen a goblin," Corranda bemoaned. "You talk about how awful and hideous they are, yet I've never seen one with my own eyes. I'd love to get a look at one of these irascible creatures."

"That's a foolish desire," Rollick scolded. "All you need to know is that goblins are wicked. They're loyal to Odjin and her only desire is to hurt others."

"Have you ever seen Odjin?" Corranda asked.

"This is fruitless talk," Rollick replied gruffly, doing his best to ignore the question. "You best get together your belongings, Corra. We leave first thing in the morning."

"Yes, Uncle," Corranda said, disappointed that she could not encourage the man to tell her more tales from his youth.

The next day Corranda and Rollick embarked on their trip. They traveled light, leaving Jumba behind to graze freely in the meadows near the cottage. They went deep into the forest and after several days they began to notice a change in the land. The trees were taller and the undergrowth more dense. There were more animals, too, for they could hear their snorts and growls, and even caught glimpses of their eyes glowing in the dark, shadowy bushes.

"Why, Corra," Rollick exclaimed on the third evening of their trip, "we just may be the only people to have ever traveled this far into the forest!"

The next morning, Corranda awoke with a strange feeling. She felt as if someone was calling her, but at the same time the sound seemed to be coming from deep within herself. She rose and dressed and, without so much as a word, left her tent and began walking through the forest grove.

Rollick had risen early to cut wood for their campfire and he noticed the girl's peculiar behavior. "Corra, where are you going?" he asked, but Corranda did not answer. Rollick was already losing sight of her, so he quickly went in pursuit.

Corranda was moving so fast that Rollick could barely keep up on his short, stubby legs. Finally, after almost an hour of brisk travel, the girl stopped, her path blocked by a giant curtain of lush green leaves.

Rollick came up behind her, breathing hard. He could

not see what was behind the wall of leaves, but he was glad for the rest. "Corra!" the dwarf panted, leaning heavily on the handle of his axe. "What has possessed you?"

Corranda seemed oblivious to the question. She stared firmly ahead at the curtain of tangled leaves, but it appeared their way was blocked. Then, as Corranda reached out, the leaves seemed to magically part, revealing the most amazing sight either of them had ever encountered: a single tree so enormous that it seemed as if it could not be real.

The tree stood within a hidden hollow in the forest, concealed by the mountain clouds and the very wall of leaves and shrubbery that only moments before had blocked their passing. Many of these leaves were the tree's own, on branches that spanned outward to create a giant canopy over the entire hollow.

Corranda now moved towards the trunk of the tree, still locked in some sort of strange trance. Rollick hurried after her, his scientific mind working eagerly to estimate the size of the great tree. All he could be sure of was that it was taller than any structure man had ever built. Indeed, the tree seemed to stretch to the very heavens, spiraling upwards in a dizzying array of limbs and leaves that disappeared into the misty clouds, high above the ceiling of the forest.

As Corranda and Rollick neared the center of the vale they realized that their initial awe at the tree's sheer size had blinded them to its true enchantment. For now, as they approached the colossal trunk, they could see that the tree was teeming with animals and birds of every kind, all of which appeared to be living in complete harmony with one another. There were creatures large and small, some carnivores, others plant eaters, some predators, and others prey. Even so, not one animal raised a claw at another, nor bore fangs in attack or defense.

Birds of every color and size perched side by side in the branches of the tree—falcons, wrens, woodpeckers, and crows—everywhere Corranda and Rollick looked they spotted a different species, some they had never seen before. Many a limb cradled a nest with eggs or chicks, and the tree resonated with the soft peeping of its fledgling inhabitants. Squirrels and mice scampered around the trunk, darting in and out of hollows and knotholes that they shared freely with cats, kestrels, and even snakes. More animals thrived at the base of the tree, amidst a network of roots and a carpet of lush forest ivy. Here rabbits, hedgehogs, lizards and ground squirrels lived in burrows alongside weasels, foxes, and badgers, their otherwise common enemies! A small lake lapped up against one side of the tree, its crystal waters supporting a host of water dwellers, including otters, turtles, frogs and a wide variety of fish. Still other, larger animals including deer, bears, and wild boars had come to rest in the cool shade provided by the gigantic tree. Every nook and cranny, every branch, seemed to house another creature!

"This is the most spectacular thing I have ever seen!" Rollick declared as a squirrel scurried over his boot. "None of these animals are fighting or attacking each other! They aren't frightened at all, not even of us!"

Corranda was still spellbound by the tree and did not respond to the dwarf's exclamation. Inexplicably, the tree was calling to her. Slowly, and almost against her will,

Corranda placed her hand upon the gigantic trunk. As she did so, the tree's inhabitants paused to look at her; the rabbits perked their ears with anticipation, the fish jumped from the lake in high arcs, and many of the birds beat their wings with excitement. As Corranda ran her palm over the course bark she felt an incredible sensation rushing through her veins, as if the tree were flooding her entire body with song and infinite joy. She had never felt such peace and happiness; she felt as if she could hear, see and feel every living thing in the forest. It was as if she could hear their thoughts; it was as if they were speaking to her!

Then something nudged against Corranda's leg, and she turned to find a fox sitting by her side, a stout branch clenched between its teeth.

"I think this peculiar creature wants you to take his stick!" Rollick told the girl.

Corranda reached down and accepted the fox's offering and, to her surprise, discovered that the branch resonated with the same mysterious power as the tree itself.

"Have you ever heard of this place?" Corranda asked her uncle. They were the first words she had spoken the entire morning.

"Never," the dwarf replied. "I thought I knew all the tales and legends told of Kendar, but never have I heard of this enchanted tree!"

"What should we do?" Corranda wondered,

slowly walking around the base of the tree, staring up into its endless network of limbs and leaves.

"This is a magical, holy place, for certain," Rollick said. "It called you here, Corra, for some strange purpose that I do not yet understand. But that branch seems to be a gift from the tree itself, so perhaps that is a clue to the mystery."

"I think we should go now," Corranda said. "It's so peaceful here, but, somehow, I do not think this place was meant for humans."

"I agree," Rollick said. "We should not overstay our welcome."

As they left, the great curtain of leaves closed up behind them, sealing the hollow. It was as though they had never even passed through the mysterious portal. As Corranda and Rollick returned to their campsite, their minds and hearts filled with great bewilderment. Rollick had always known Corranda was special—she was a princess, after all—but now it seemed she possessed a mysterious power.

That night, sitting at the fire, Rollick had an inspiration about the magic tree. He was sure that Corranda was meant to use the branch somehow and so, through the next two days and nights, the old dwarf worked at the piece of wood, whittling it with the slow and methodical movement of his knife. When he started, he was not sure what he was carving. It seemed as if the branch itself was controlling his motions, letting its secret form emerge from the wood, shaving by shaving.

When Rollick finally put down his knife, he had created something wondrous—a musical pipe carved from the single piece of wood.

"Uncle Rollick!" Corranda exclaimed when she saw the

pipe. "It's beautiful!"

"Give it a try," Rollick urged. "Let's hear its sound."

Corranda put the pipe to her lips, and suddenly she felt a great communion with all the creatures of the forest—the same feeling she had experienced at the enchanted tree itself!

As she played the pipe the woodland creatures appeared out of the brush and began to speak to her. To Rollick the sounds were nothing more than barks, hoots and yowls, but to Corranda the words were clear.

"Korr-an-rah! Korr-an-rah!" the animals chanted. "Can you hear us?"

"Yes, I can hear you!" Corranda exclaimed, taking the pipe from her mouth. "But why do you call me 'Korr-an-rah'? My name is Corra!"

"We have always called you that," a long-legged hare explained. "In our language it means 'One-Who-Is-Kind-To-The-Earth'!"

"How could you have called me this?" Corranda asked, scratching her head with confusion. "I have never spoken with animals before!"

"But we have spoken of you!" a whiskery otter said. "The stories of your kindness to the animals and birds are told throughout the forest!"

"Oh!" Corranda said. "I had no idea!"

"Can you actually understand these creatures?" Rollick asked Corranda in astonishment.

"Yes, as plain as day!" Corranda replied.

"What are they saying?!" Rollick cried in puzzlement.

"Hello, I guess!" the girl told him.

"Amazing," Rollick murmured.

Upon returning to the cottage, the old dwarf fashioned a leather cord so that Corranda could wear the pipe around her neck. As long as she was wearing the pipe, Corranda found that she could understand and speak to all the creatures in the forest. And, if she played the pipe, she could command any animal or bird to do exactly as she wished. Of course, this was a privilege she never abused. At most she would ask one of her tree-climbing friends to pick her an apple or berry which was too high up for her to reach.

Corranda was friendly with all the woodland dwellers, but her closest companions were Orufoo the fox, Kapoora the otter, and Shutakee the crow. These three were never far from Corranda's side, whether she was doing her daily chores or just daydreaming underneath the willow tree that grew by the brook. Corranda had never had friends or playmates while growing up. Now, it seemed, the entire forest population had befriended her.

Chapter 7

✿

Corranda's Animal Education

ow that she could speak with them, it was only natural that Corranda came to better understand the creatures living in the forest. She had an avid curiosity and wanted to learn everything she could about animal instincts, habitats, and their way of life. She plied Orufoo, Kapoora, and Shutakee with dozens of questions.

"Animal names are very strange to me," Corranda mentioned to her friends one sunny afternoon as they were sitting on the bank of the brook. "Do they mean anything?"

"Of course," Orufoo said as he scratched one of his ears with a long hind leg. "All names mean something. Doesn't yours?"

"I don't know," Corranda confessed. "My uncle just said it was the name my mother gave me, but he didn't say if it had any significance. He doesn't really like to talk about it."

"Yes, your uncle can be very short," Orufoo declared.

"Of course he's short," Shutakee cawed from her nearby perch. "He's a dwarf, after all."

"But I meant short on patience too," Orufoo explained with a smirk. "Don't you get it? That's part of the joke."

"It's a bad joke," Shutakee retorted, ruffling her feathers. She was a loud bird who liked to voice her opinions, especially when it came to Orufoo's poorly-conceived puns. "Your jokes are always bad, Orufoo," the crow added.

"Why, if I were not so good-natured, I expect I would be offended by such a remark," the fox voiced.

"Perhaps you should try and work on your puns in private," Kapoora suggested. She was a soft-spoken animal and didn't care much for the constant bickering between the fox and the crow.

"That sounds like too much effort," Orufoo said, his large pink tongue hanging out the side of his mouth. "I have to live by my wits."

"It's a wonder you've lived this long," Shutakee said.

"This is all very well," Corranda interrupted, "but you still haven't told me what your names mean."

"My name means 'Swift-On-Water'," Kapoora answered, combing her whiskers with her two front paws. "It was given to me because I am an excellent swimmer, even for an otter."

"Animals and birds are not named right at birth," Shutakee told Corranda. "We must wait until we reach a certain maturity. After a time, our names are naturally revealed."

"What do you mean?" Corranda asked.

"Take my name, for instance," Shutakee said. "It means 'Iron-Beak.' After I was a few weeks old, it became apparent that I had a harder, sharper beak than any of my brothers or sisters. One day, when I was still just a fledgling, I pecked at a stone and split it right in two. As soon as my mother saw this, she knew what my name should be."

"I guess the only thing sharper than your beak, Shutakee, is your tongue," Orufoo jested.

"You'd like to think so," Shutakee replied. "If I didn't know better, I'd say your name meant 'Bad-Joke'."

Orufoo stuck his tongue out at the bird. "Of course that's not what my name means," the fox said good-naturedly.

"It means 'Laughing-Snout'."

Corranda understood immediately why Orufoo had been given such a name. He had a long crooked grin that gave him a very comical appearance and made it seem as if he was always on the verge of laughing.

"Your name is very fitting," Corranda said.

The subject of animal names was a very interesting one to Corranda. Everyday she seemed to learn something new about the animal kingdom and she was coming to understand that it was a far more mysterious and intricate world than she had ever imagined.

That night, as she was brushing out Jumba's long coat, Corranda asked the cow about her name.

"My name doesn't mean anything," Jumba told the girl. "At least not in the language of animals. It was given to me by the farmer who raised me before he sold me to your uncle."

"So Jumba's your human name," Corranda said, leaning over to inspect a burr which was entangled in the cow's hair. "But don't you have an animal name too?"

"If I do, I never learned it," Jumba replied. "It's different for domestic animals, Corra."

"Why?" Corranda asked, as she gently pulled the burr from the cow's coat.

"Because domestic animals are not wild and free like Orufoo, Shutakee, and Kapoora," Jumba explained. "We are owned by humans; they're the ones who name us."

"Oh," Corranda said, pressing her head close to the neck of the giant cow. "Doesn't that sadden you?"

"I guess not," Jumba replied. "I don't think I ever really thought about it. Jumba's the only name I have ever known!"

"Well, it's not such a bad name after all," Corranda said, hanging the brush up on a peg on the wall. "Good night, Jumba."

"Good night, Corra," the cow lowed.

Corranda hummed a quiet song to herself as she danced across the dark lawn to the cottage. Inside, her uncle was carving an ornate decoration into the back of a rocking chair. Corranda meant to ask him again about the meaning of her name, but at the last minute decided against it, and instead went quietly to bed.

Chapter 8

১৩

A Trip to Town

*A*ny feelings of loneliness that Corranda had experienced earlier in her life were gone, yet her restlessness was not. She craved adventure and romance and longed to leave the tiny cottage in the forest for the wider experiences of the world. Rollick was not oblivious to the girl's discontent; it was a troubling time for him, as he knew that the moment was fast approaching when he would have to reveal to Corranda her true identity. Yet the old dwarf lingered in this duty, for he loved the girl dearly and was afraid of the dangers that awaited her in the world.

At last, going against his better judgment, Rollick decided to let Corranda accompany him on his annual spring journey into Cobald to buy food, tools, and other supplies. He was beset with fear that Odjin's goblins would discover Corranda's identity, but he knew he could not hide the girl forever.

"Can I bring Orufoo, Kapoora, and Shutakee?" Corranda asked excitedly on the morning of the trip.

"I don't see much reason for them to come," Rollick replied gruffly. "People will think it's pretty strange for a girl to have wild animals as pets."

"They're not pets—they're my friends," Corranda said.

"Yes, I know that," Rollick said with frustration. "But it will draw attention to us."

"Well, they don't have to come into the town itself," Corranda pressed. "Can they at least come for the trip?"

"Oh, very well," Rollick said, throwing his hands up in the air. "I suppose you will pester me until I agree anyway!"

"Thank you, Uncle!" Corranda said, kissing the old man on his forehead. She whisked off to pack a few belongings for the trip, leaving Rollick to shake his head.

They traveled to Cobald by means of a wagon cart hitched to Jumba. The journey passed without event, though Rollick worried the entire time about goblins. Despite his anxiety, they encountered no one on the road, and after a day and a half they rolled into the small vale where Cobald sat nestled alongside the Uka River.

Rollick stopped the wagon on a hillside just outside of Cobald and the small band of travelers clambered onto the grass to stretch their legs and gaze upon the town. Corranda

could see the town bustling with activity.

"I can't wait to start exploring the village!" Corranda proclaimed excitedly.

"Don't forget, we're leaving the animals here!" Rollick reminded her.

"Very well," Corranda said, turning to her friends. "Will you three be all right by yourselves?"

"Of course," Orufoo barked indignantly. "We're animals, after all!"

"On your way back, just call us with your pipe," Shutakee told Corranda. "That way we'll know how to find you."

With these preparations made, Corranda and Rollick climbed back into the wagon and set off down the hill towards Cobald.

"Now you mind yourself, Corra," Rollick told the girl. "I have to run some errands about town and you're free to roam the market. Just stay out of any trouble!"

"Of course!" Corranda said. "What possible trouble could I get into?"

"Well, just don't go talking to any of the pigs in the market!" Rollick said. "Remember, it may be natural for you to talk to animals, but everyone else will think it's strange."

"I'll behave," Corranda promised.

Once they entered the village, Corranda hopped off the wagon and let Rollick and Jumba go about on their way. Her heart beat with excitement as she wandered through the streets, gathering in all the sights, sounds, and smells.

There seemed to be all manner of goods for sale in the

little stalls that lined the streets. Some merchants plied the townspeople with spices, food, and ale, while others had pottery, pans, and a variety of cooking implements for sale. Still others showcased shoes, cloaks, and other garments.

As Corranda meandered through the square she came upon an old beggar woman sitting in the street, lonely and dejected. She was thin and pale and her clothes were ragged and patched.

"Are you all right, miss?" Corranda asked, crouching down to talk to the woman.

"I am just a poor old beggar, looking for something to eat," the woman mumbled.

"Here, I have something for you," Corranda said, digging into her pouch. She found some cheese and a bit of bread, which she gave to the woman.

"Thank you," the woman said, gladly taking the food. "My name is Zolga. Who are you?"

"I'm Corra," the girl offered. "Nice to meet you, Zolga."

"Same to you," Zolga said. "I have never seen you in the village before. You're not from around here, are you?"

"No, I live in the forest with my uncle," Corranda explained.

"Myself, I have lived in this village all my life," Zolga declared.

"How come no one else has come to help you?" Corranda asked. She had never witnessed poverty before and was shocked by the woman's poor condition.

"Times have been hard," Zolga explained. "People can barely spare enough food for their own families, let alone help a poor old beggar woman."

"Don't you have any family of your own?" Corranda inquired.

"I had a son," Zolga said sadly. "Then the blight came to our farm and destroyed all of our crops. My son went south to look for work, but he never came back. They say Odjin turned him into a goblin."

"A goblin!?" Corranda cried.

"Yes," Zolga said. "They say that's how the goblins come to be. All it takes is one look from the witch's cruel eyes and she can turn you into one of those horrid beasts. He was a handsome man, my son, and the stories claim that Odjin is jealous of anyone who might compete with her own beauty. You should be wary too, child. You have your own beauty. If Odjin was to see you, she might grow jealous and decide to turn you into a goblin too."

"Oh, I don't expect she'd come all the way to our tiny little cottage in the woods," Corranda remarked.

"No, probably not," Zolga agreed. "Not unless you were the lost princess, of course. She would go to the ends of the earth for her. You're not she, are you?

"Lost princess!" Corranda exclaimed. "I don't even know what you're talking about!"

"The legend of the lost princess of Kendar!" Zolga cried with astonishment. "Everyone knows that story!"

"Not me," Corranda admitted with a sigh. "My uncle's not much for telling stories. Tell me about it, Zolga."

The old woman laughed, a slight twinkle in her eye. The meager meal she had been provided seemed to do wonders for her strength, as did Corranda's company. "I will tell you," Zolga chuckled. "Though I would think you're a little old for fairy tales!"

"Tell me anyway," Corranda urged.

"Almost fifteen years ago now, Odjin the Beautiful and her army of goblins waged a battle against Kendar," Zolga began. "King Daron and Queen Anya were destroyed, but legend has it that they entrusted their infant daughter to one of their servants so that she might be smuggled to safety. Where she was taken, no one knows. Where she hides, no one knows. They say one day the princess shall return to free Kendar from the witch. But perhaps it's just a story after all. Perhaps the princess perished long ago, with her parents. Still, it's the only hope we have."

Corranda's mind was racing with excitement. She could not help but dream that she herself was the lost princess of Kendar. Maybe she was not a simple peasant girl after all, doomed to live out her life in the confines of the forest. Perhaps her life held greater adventure yet.

"But how will you know the princess when she comes?" Corranda wondered.

"They say she is marked by a symbol," Zolga explained. "A birthmark or some blemish on her body that looks like a tiny crown. Some say this mark is on her neck, some on her hand . . . still others say it's on her forehead, plain as day!" Zolga could see that the girl was deep in thought. "I suppose you are wondering if you have such a mark on your own body?" the old woman asked.

"I suppose every girl has imagined that she was the lost princess at some time or other," Corranda admitted, red in the face. "Still, I have no mark upon my face or neck, as you can plainly see yourself."

"Just as well, child," Zolga told Corranda, putting her

arm around the girl. "You do not want to be the object of Odjin's envy and hatred. She obliterates everything that stands in her way."

Corranda leaned over and hugged the woman. "Thank you for the story, Zolga," she said kindly. "I guess I better be on my way. I hope you see your son again."

Zolga nodded with sadness. Corranda rose and shuffled back into the crowd. She suddenly had a bad feeling, and a shiver went down her spine. There was something not quite right in the village, she decided, but she wasn't sure what it could be. She stopped in the middle of the square, but could see nothing out of the ordinary. She had just decided her imagination was playing a trick on her when she heard the first loud crash.

Chapter 9

❧

Goblin Encounters

Orufoo was still sitting with his two friends on the grassy hillside just outside of Cobald when he caught scent of the goblins. He suddenly rose on all fours, his fur bristling with warning.

"Goblins!" the fox growled. "I'd know their foul stench anywhere!"

"You've smelt them before?" Kapoora asked.

"Yes, they've ventured into the forest before to hunt," Orufoo replied. "On a clear night you can smell them from the other side of the woods." He paused to sniff again at the air, wriggling his nose with disgust as he did so. "It's them all right!" he declared. "The nose knows! Get it—I 'nose' it!"

"Yes, yes," Kapoora said impatiently. "This is hardly the time for jokes!"

Just then the goblins came into view. There were at least two dozen of the vile creatures, and they were headed right into Cobald, led by a fat hairy goblin on a black horse.

Without a second thought, Orufoo bounded down the hill towards town.

"Orufoo, wait!" Kapoora called after the fox. "You can't just go storming into a man village!"

The fox paused to look back at his friends. "Corra's in

there!" Orufoo barked. "Village or not, we can't leave her to those wretched beasts!"

"Then we'll all go!" Shutakee cawed, and she and the otter chased after their companion.

By the time they reached the village, it was in complete chaos, with people screaming and shouting as they scrambled to escape the attacking goblins. With all the confusion and panic, no one had any time to bother about the animals who had come right into the center of the mayhem to search for their human friend.

"I don't see her anywhere!" Shutakee shouted, fluttering over the crowd.

"Keep looking!" Kapoora cried, doing her best not to get trampled.

Corranda herself was engaged in a desperate search of her own, looking frantically about the village square for her uncle. Search as she might, she could find no trace of the small man amidst the panicked throng.

A sharp, sudden crack brought her to a halt, and Corranda whirled around to see her uncle being chased by a goblin on horseback with a long leather whip. In his haste to escape, Rollick stumbled to the ground, and with a malicious cackle, the goblin reared his horse above the dwarf, ready to trample him!

"Little man gonna get squishy!" the goblin shrieked with a big, crooked grin.

If she had been close enough, Corranda would have thrown herself before her uncle without a second thought, but there was no way she could get through the crowd in time. Desperately, Corranda reached for her pipe and quickly brought it to her lips. She did not think of the consequences of beckoning her power in such a public place. Her only thoughts were of saving her uncle, and she instantly filled the square with music, a loud and enchanting sound that cut through the commotion and commanded the goblin's horse to leave Rollick unharmed. Compelled by Corranda's song, the horse immediately lowered his hooves and backed away from Rollick.

The goblin was furious at his horse's insolence. "Squishy little man!" the goblin ordered, whipping the animal.

The horse was torn between the goblin's anger and Corranda's song. As the goblin whipped him once more, Corranda's pipe called out to the horse in a peaceful melody, and the animal suddenly decided that he would rid himself of his vile master once and for all. With a furious buck, he sent the goblin sailing off his back and hurtling onto the street!

The entire square seemed to come to a halt as the people

stopped and stared at Corranda. No one could be entirely sure what had happened, but one thing was for certain: the sound of the girl's pipe had somehow saved the dwarf's life.

As for the goblin, he was too consumed by rage to grasp the significance of Corranda's magic. Pulling

himself from the dust, the deformed creature stared across the street to see who had been the cause of his misfortune.

Now this was no ordinary goblin, but the wretched Captain Wort who had spent the last fifteen years scouring the land for the missing princess. Upon seeing Corranda, Wort's eyes instantly narrowed with suspicion. The goblin had been to countless villages and towns, and had ransacked every farm up and down the river, yet the princess had somehow eluded him. Could this, at last, be the legendary Corranda of Kendar?

"You girly!" he yelled, pointing a long crooked finger at Corranda. "Come here!"

Rollick, still lying in the street, looked up in panic. His

greatest fear had come to pass, for Rollick knew that any close inspection by the goblin would reveal Corranda's mark, and her identity.

"No!" Rollick cried, trying to pull himself to his feet. "Run, Corra! Run!"

"Silence, dwarfy!" Wort snarled. "You under arresty!"

Corranda gasped with fright and quickly moved through the market to aid her uncle.

"You stay away from him!" she yelled.

Corranda suddenly felt a tug on her cloak and she looked down to see Kapoora pulling at her with her teeth. Orufoo and Shutakee were there too, for they had all heard her pipe.

"Listen to me, child!" Kapoora cried desperately. "You cannot win against the goblins now!"

"There's only one of them!" Corranda retorted, but when she looked up she suddenly noticed a dozen of the beasts pushing their way through the crowd towards her. They were armed with axes and swords, and their large eyes gleamed with hatred.

"Seize that girly!" Wort screamed to his henchmen.

Corranda froze, helpless. She was consumed with terror and wanted to flee, yet she could not abandon her uncle.

"You cannot save him now!" Kapoora warned. "If you stay you will only be captured too—then what help can you be to him!?"

Corranda stared across the street at her uncle, still lying in a crumpled heap before Captain Wort.

"Go!" the old dwarf commanded. "Don't worry for me, Corra! You must escape!"

Wort grabbed Rollick by the scruff of his neck and with

his large scaly hand clamped the old man's mouth shut. But Rollick's words had already broken Corranda's spell and she turned to hide in the crowd, just as one of the goblins got hold of her with his bony claws.

"Me gotcha, girly!" the goblin hissed.

Then suddenly Shutakee dived down from the sky and gave the goblin a piercing blow with her sharp beak. With a deafening wail, the slimy creature reeled into the mud, still clutching a piece of Corranda's cloak.

Corranda needed no further warning. She turned and fled through the square, her three friends fast at her side. Wort's soldiers followed in hot pursuit, screaming and hurling spears.

With a loud twang, one of the spears whistled over Kapoora's head, just missing her.

"We've got to get into the woods!" the otter exclaimed.

"I 'wood' agree!" Orufoo said. "Get it? I mean 'wood' instead of 'would'!"

"Just go!" Kapoora cried impatiently.

They raced down a side street until they reached the outskirts of the village. Still the goblins pursued them, through the fields and over the hills that surrounded Cobald. Corranda was exhausted, but she knew even a moment's pause would mean her capture. Finally, she and her friends reached the protection of the woods, and the girl allowed herself a sigh of relief. Corranda was now in her own element. She understood the forest. She knew where to hide and how to cover her tracks so as to disguise her passing. The goblins, on the other hand, were recklessly loud and could be heard crashing through the dense foliage.

"Listen to that racket!" Shutakee remarked. "It sounds like they're hacking down the entire forest!"

"At least we know they won't sneak up on us," Corranda declared. "Let's hide in one of these trees. They probably won't think to look for us up there!"

Orufoo and Kapoora were not natural climbers and Corranda had to help them as they ascended the nearest tree. They were soon so far above the ground that everyone except Shutakee became dizzy just by looking down.

Just then the goblins came charging into the hollow, stopping right beneath their hiding place.

"Dreadful beasts!" Shutakee cawed.

"Stop!" one of the goblins cried suddenly. "You hears something, Lieutenant Meezle?"

"No, that just Wreek," the tall skinny goblin named Meezle replied. "He make stinky!"

"Me no stinky!" the goblin called Wreek protested.

"You doos too!" Meezle retorted. "Now let's get move on. Wort no like it if we come back without girly!"

With that, the goblins moved off through the woods, noisy as ever. Corranda suddenly realized she had been holding her breath with anxiety during the entire goblin conversation, and finally exhaled.

"Great crowing, Shutakee!" Orufoo barked. "You nearly blew it for us!"

"No fighting now!" Corranda warned. "We have to figure out what to do!"

"We must be careful," Kapoora advised. "Those goblins will tear down the forest looking for us!"

"But what about Uncle Rollick?" Corranda asked. "I need to know if he's okay! What do you think they'll do with him?"

"I don't know," Shutakee said. "Most prisoners are taken before the witch. But it's a long way to her castle from here."

"I'm going to rescue him," Corranda declared with determination.

"Easy, child," Kapoora said. "You can't just go rushing after him. Besides, it'll be night in a few hours. The best thing to do is get some rest—it's been quite a day!"

"Kapoora's right," Shutakee said. "First thing in the morning, I will fly into town and see if I can find anything out about your uncle."

Corranda could not argue with her friends' logic. She was exhausted from their escape and meant to sleep right in the tree, safe from the goblins' probing eyes. She had no food left, so there would be no dinner, but she did have a bit of rope in her pouch which she used to tie herself to the tree so that she would not fall to the ground in her sleep.

"Well," Orufoo said, observing the girl as she knotted herself to the tree trunk, "I guess that's one way to sleep tight!"

Chapter 10

ঔও

Manchipukoo's News

T rue to her word, Shutakee departed early the next morning to seek out news about Rollick, leaving her friends behind in the safety of the tree. Corranda, Orufoo, and Kapoora groaned as they stretched gingerly in the warm sun, their muscles sore and stiff from spending the night in the tree's hard branches.

"Can you still smell those goblins?" Corranda asked Orufoo.

"Their stink is so strong, I think I'll have their stench in my fur for days," Orufoo said. "But I don't think they're anywhere near right now. Let's get out of this tree!"

The three friends eagerly returned to the familiarity of the forest floor. Corranda found a spring and after a wash and drink, made a small breakfast from a nearby blackberry bush.

After a few hours, Shutakee returned.

"There's not much left of Cobald," the crow informed them. "I spoke with Urjeepa the wren, and she says that fat goblin's temper really exploded after we escaped. His name is Wort, and apparently he's the captain of the entire goblin army!"

"What would the captain of Odjin's army be doing all

the way up here?" Kapoora wondered.

"I don't know," Shutakee said. "But he has an appetite for destruction, I can tell you that. He looted the entire town, and trampled most of the houses and farmsteads to rubble! He took everything he could get his filthy claws on—he even took old Jumba!"

"They got Jumba?" Corranda cried. "What about my uncle? Did you see him?"

"Not myself," Shutakee replied. "Urjeepa says Captain Wort loaded up all his loot in a bunch of wagons and headed out of town last night. He took your uncle with him."

"But to where?" Corranda asked.

"They're heading south," Shutakee said. "My guess is that Wort's taking his plunder to the witch."

"But what do they want with Uncle Rollick?" Corranda

wondered. "He's just a poor old woodsman!"

"Maybe Odjin orders all prisoners to be brought before her," Orufoo suggested.

"She'll turn him into a goblin!" Corranda cried.

"Try not to worry, Corra," Kapoora comforted. "You don't know that for sure."

"How many goblins are in this caravan heading south?" Orufoo asked the crow.

"At least a dozen," Shutakee replied. "Wort has left some of his goblins behind to keep searching for Corra. I expect more will come."

"Not even the forest will be safe from them for very long," Orufoo muttered. "What should we do now, Corra?"

"There's only one thing I can do," the girl said. "I'm going after Uncle Rollick."

"I don't know how we can take on an entire goblin troop," Orufoo said skeptically.

"I'm not asking you to come with me," Corranda told her friends. "It's too dangerous."

"Sweet child," Kapoora murmured, rubbing against her leg. "We go where you go, dangerous or not."

"This will be a long journey," Corranda warned. "I fear we will have to travel all the way to the castle itself."

"Don't worry about us," Shutakee said. "We mean to come with you, whether you allow it or not!"

Corranda could see that their minds were made up. In truth, she was relieved. She was frightened of the road that lay before her, and knew her friends would be helpful in the times ahead. "Very well," the girl said finally. "I'm grateful for your friendship."

The matter was settled, and Corranda realized there was no reason for delaying their start. She had nothing to pack; indeed, her only possessions were her pipe, her small traveling pouch, and the clothes she was wearing. She would have to forage for food in the forest along the way and make out the best she could.

"Well," Corranda said, "we better get a move on!"

They followed a forest trail through the dense growth of the forest and made their way south. The going was slow, but they knew that eventually their direction would lead them to intersect the main highway that Wort had taken with his goblin caravan. They spent the night in the woods again, this time in a little cave that Orufoo found at the base of a hill.

They had only been on their way for a few hours that next morning when they came upon an old friend, Manchipukoo the bear. Manchipukoo's name meant "One-Who-Walks-Heavy," for he was a giant animal who did not like to move quickly.

"Hello, my friends," the bear greeted.

"Hello, Manchipukoo!" Corranda said as she embraced the large, grizzled animal.

"Have you seen any goblins?" Orufoo asked. "C'mon—just give us the 'bear' facts?"

Manchipukoo sat down upon his massive haunches and let out a terrific yawn before eyeing the fox and giving his slow reply. "Do you still have such bad humor, Orufoo?" he asked. "It seems to me you would have outgrown it by now."

"What's it matter to you?" Orufoo inquired. "I know you come 'bearing' news—just give it to us!"

Manchipukoo groaned. "Sometimes I have half a mind

to eat you and put the forest out of its misery," he growled.

"Oh, come now," Orufoo retorted. "I don't think you could 'bear' to live without me!"

"Stop it, Orufoo!" Corranda interrupted finally. "I want

to know if Manchipukoo has heard anything about Uncle Rollick!"

"I don't know anything about your uncle," the bear stated, happy to be relieved of Orufoo's jokes. "But I saw Chukolo the owl this morning, and she told me that the goblins have swarmed the entire forest looking for you."

"Why are we so important to them?" Corranda asked.

"I don't know," Manchipukoo said. "But they mean business. They already found your cottage, Corra, and burned it to the ground in the middle of the night!"

Corranda gasped with horror. The cottage and everything in it represented her entire life, the only life she had known.

"Why would they do that!?" Corranda cried in despair.

"That's what goblins do," Manchipukoo said. "They destroy things!"

"We're lucky we didn't go back to the cottage," Kapoora said. "I fear what might have happened if we had."

"What are you going to do now?" Manchipukoo asked Corranda.

"The goblins captured Uncle Rollick and are taking him to Odjin's castle," Corranda replied. "We're going after him."

"This is a dangerous thing you try to do," Manchipukoo warned.

"I have to try and save him," Corranda said.

"I understand," Manchipukoo said wearily. "I would offer my help, Corra, but I have a she-bear and cubs to think of. With all these goblins about, these are not safe times in the forest."

"Thank you, Manchipukoo," Corranda said, hugging the

bear goodbye. "You are a true friend."

"Very well then," Manchipukoo said, rising to all fours. At such a height, he towered over Corranda and her friends. "I must be on my way. Goodbye, all, and good luck!"

With that, the giant animal turned and lumbered through the trees, slowly and heavily. Corranda watched him disappear into the woods and realized that she was crying. It seemed that her entire life had been turned upside down. One thing was certain: there was no going back. She would have to move ahead.

Chapter 11

❧

The Abandoned Farm

*L*ater that day, Corranda and her friends broke clear of the forest and found the highway. The road had once been paved with bricks, but now many parts of it had degenerated into broken patches of rubble.

"Of course, we won't be able to travel on the road itself," Kapoora said. "It's much too dangerous, what with all the goblins about."

"And there could be humans up and down the highway too," Orufoo pointed out.

"Humans are nothing to be afraid of," Corranda declared indignantly.

"Not for you, Corra," Orufoo argued. "But for animals, humans can be a grave threat. Myself, I prefer to avoid them. Other than you of course, Corra—and your uncle."

Some further discussion settled the matter, and the friends decided it would be safer to keep to the woods between the highway and the river.

"We'll be okay as long as we don't lose sight of the Uka River," Kapoora advised her friends. "It winds south all the way to the castle of Kendar and out to the Samboora Sea."

"How do you know the river?" Corranda asked. "Have you been down it before?"

"No, not I," Kapoora responded. "But I am a water dweller and part of a greater community than that of the forest. Knowledge of the Uka River is passed up and down its currents by fish, geese, and other otters, so I feel I know it as well as if I lived on it myself."

They proceeded without event for the next few weeks, and made good progress. They saw little sign of life, except from afar: the occasional fieldworker or scraggly farm animal. Still, they kept their distance, and Shutakee often flew ahead of the group to act as a lookout for trouble.

Late one afternoon, the small band of travelers came across an old, abandoned farm, and they decided that it would be a good place to camp the night. The farmhouse

had long ago been destroyed, but the barn was mostly intact, and Corranda welcomed the thought of having a roof, or at least part of one, over her head.

"I imagine it was goblins that caused such chaos here," Shutakee remarked as she looked over the shattered remains of the farm.

Corranda explored the area and discovered an old apple tree and a field of corn which had grown back again despite the lack of cultivation. These made a decent enough dinner, which she supplemented with some wild roots and acorns.

The animals fended for themselves when it came to eating, and while Corranda gathered her dinner, Kapoora and Shutakee disappeared to the river and Orufoo prowled into the woods for a night hunt.

"Doesn't it bother you to hunt other creatures?" Corranda asked the fox when the animals had returned and they were all resting in the ramshackle barn.

"It's the way of foxes," Orufoo commented casually. "I must hunt in order to survive."

"I don't think I could ever hunt," Corranda remarked.

"You might," Shutakee argued. "If you were a fox, then it would be in your nature."

"Then I would starve, I guess," Corranda decided. "I'm not a meat eater."

"It's the way of the wild, Corra," Kapoora explained. "Some animals are carnivores and must hunt. All living things depend on each other for life—even humans."

"What about goblins?" Corranda asked. "They're living things too."

"Have you ever taken a good whiff of one of those

mongrels?" Orufoo asked. "I don't know how anything that smells so awful can be considered alive!"

"Goblins were never meant to be," Kapoora said. "They are aberrations of nature, created by Odjin's dark powers. They have tilted the very balance of the land."

"It's true," Shutakee agreed. "I don't know what will become of us, humans and animals both, if these goblins are left to run rampant. They are exhausting the land with their feeding and their filth. Soon there will be nothing left."

"Well, this is enough serious talk," Orufoo declared. He disappeared around the corner and returned wearing a bucket upon his head. He couldn't see a thing, and bumped into every obstacle in his path.

Corranda could not help but laugh at the fox's antics. "Orufoo, what are you doing?" she giggled.

"Just trying to lighten up this dismal affair!" the fox

replied. "Gee, I feel so 'pail'! Do you get it—'pail' and 'pale' both!"

Shutakee groaned and was just about to comment on Orufoo's poor pun when the fox suddenly whirled about and growled.

"What is it!?" Corranda exclaimed.

"Don't you smell it?" the fox asked, still wearing the battered bucket. "The wind just shifted! I smell goblins!"

With a gasp, Corranda jumped to her feet, but in a matter of seconds there seemed to be goblins in every corner of the barn, and the girl found herself surrounded.

Orufoo could not see a thing with the bucket on his head and instantly panicked. He zigzagged across the floor like a crazed creature, plowing through goblins as he went. The frightened fox had no idea where he was going and eventually charged right into a wall with such force that he fell back to his haunches, dazed and confused. He finally shook

the pail from his head, but experienced freedom for only a few fleeting seconds before a heavy sack was thrown over his body. Orufoo snapped and growled feverishly at his captors, but he could not bite through the thick sack.

Shutakee soared to the fox's aid, but before the crow knew what had happened, she found herself lying on the floor in a crumpled heap, entangled in the fine mesh of a goblin's net.

Kapoora alone had managed to evade the goblins' traps, and she knew if she was to be of any help to her friends, she would have to use her brains, not her brawn. Looking about quickly, Kapoora found a length of rope coiled on the floor, one end of it tied to a rusted metal loop in the wall of the barn. Kapoora grabbed the loose end between her teeth and ran straight into the bevy of goblins who surrounded Corranda. The otter darted in and out between their crooked legs, entangling them as she went. As the rope came to its end, it suddenly became taut, and the goblins tumbled to the floor in a heap of hairy bodies and twisted limbs.

"Come on, Corra!" Kapoora yelled. "Let's get out of here!"

Corranda scrambled over the pile of fallen goblins, even as more of the dreadful creatures scurried towards her. She desperately wanted to help Orufoo and Shutakee, but some of the goblins had already whisked them away into the woods. Corranda regretfully realized she would have to leave her friends behind, at least for now.

Kapoora was already on the run, scampering through a broken section of the barn wall and towards the Uka River. Corranda quickly turned and caught up to the otter.

"All we have to do is make it to the water!" Kapoora panted, as the goblins spilled out of the barn after them. "Those wretched demons can't swim, and won't dare follow us into the river!"

Goblin arrows and spears zinged past the two friends as they raced down the river embankment and plunged head-first into the water. Feeling the swift cold water engulf her body, Corranda came to the surface and gulped for air. The current was strong, and Corranda felt completely helpless as she was pulled downstream. Bobbing up and down in the water, she looked back and saw that Kapoora had been right about the goblins. They had ended their pursuit at the riverbank, too afraid to enter the water. She even saw one of the goblins dip his toe into the water, only to recoil with a fearful shiver.

The persistent pests weren't about to give up entirely, however, and Corranda and Kapoora suddenly found themselves besieged by a shower of spears, arrows, and rocks as the goblins began hurling every object they could find.

"Keep you head down, child!" Kapoora shouted over the roar of the river. "We'll be out of a range in a moment!"

The otter had barely finished her sentence, however, when one of the goblins' stones hit Corranda squarely in the head. The girl felt a surge of pain down her neck, and then everything went black. As she slipped into unconsciousness, her motionless body slowly sank into the cold grip of the river.

Chapter 12

✂

Rollick's Fate

C aptain Wort had wasted no time in making a decision regarding his new prisoner, Rollick the Dwarf. The plump goblin clearly remembered that it had been a dwarf who had escaped with the princess all those years ago; he wasn't sure if this was the same dwarf, but he wasn't going to take any chances. He planned to take Rollick directly to Odjin so that the witch herself could interrogate his captive.

So, after looting Cobald of every possible object of worth, Wort put the old dwarf in chains and embarked on the long journey to Odjin's castle.

Wort's wagon loads of plunder included not only money and jewelry, but food, livestock, and even the crude wooden furniture which his goblin ruffians had found in the humble homes of Cobald's citizens. Wort, of course, didn't need the furniture, but he was lazy and didn't like to chop firewood when it came to building his nightly campfires. It would be much easier to burn the stolen furniture.

As they traveled south on the highway, Wort did his best to engage Rollick in conversation, hoping that the dwarf would reveal something about his true identity.

"You little dwarfy who hide Princess?" Wort asked the first night as they set up camp on the side of the road.

Rollick sighed and shifted uncomfortably in his shackles. Wort would not release him from the chains, not even temporarily so that he could eat or sleep without constraint.

"How come you no talky me, dwarf?" Wort demanded, poking the old man with a bony finger. "You no like talky me?"

"No, I don't want to talk to you," Rollick said in exasperation. "I don't like to talk to goblins! I don't like your kind at all!"

"That's hearty har-har," Wort giggled with malevolent delight. "Soon you see Odjin. She looky you right in the eye. She make you just like me."

"Is that how she does it?" Rollick asked, regarding the horrible creature with curiosity.

"Yes, yes!" Wort replied with a dreamy expression. "Once you sees her, you falls in love. Then you not be so glum! You be happy as a birdy-bird!"

Rollick very much doubted the goblin's claim. "Then you were a human once?" he inquired.

"Yes, me once ugly humany thing," Wort spat with disgust. "Ugh! Ugly creature just like dwarfy!"

"What was your name?" Rollick asked.

"Me Wort," the ugly goblin replied simply.

"No, I mean your other name, your human name," Rollick said. "You must have had a human name before you became a goblin."

"Me Wort now," the goblin declared. "No remember human name. No care either. No remember much before being in love with Odjin."

"Bah!" Rollick retorted. "That isn't love! It's just an enchantment! She certainly doesn't love you!"

"Yes she do!" Wort cried angrily, jumping up and jabbing Rollick again with his scraggly claw. "You sees it all right, dwarfy! Odjin purtiest woman in whole world. You falls in love with her too!"

With that, the vile beast stormed off, leaving Rollick alone to contemplate the painful chafing of his heavy chains against his skin.

Chapter 13

ঙৄ

Odjin's Beauty

ar to the south, in the castle of Kendar, Odjin the Beautiful looked down upon the landscape of her conquered country from a tall, dark tower, and she brooded. She had no idea that Captain Wort had captured Rollick the Dwarf, the vital link to the long-lost Princess Corranda. Still, despite the passing of fifteen years, the royal child consumed Odjin's mind. As far as she was concerned, her revenge would not be complete until she captured Daron's daughter.

The sorceress watched as night descended upon the countryside that surrounded the somber castle. As the long black shadows stretched across the villages and farms, Odjin could hear the odd, desolate sounds emanating from the valley; the thin, distant barking of a sheep dog or the lonely wail of a milk cow as it hoofed home to its stable after a day of poor grazing. With a sigh, Odjin turned her eyes from the countryside to the darkening sky.

The land was dying.

She had known it for a long time, though she could not explain it, could not stop it. Even if she knew how to halt the drought that plagued Kendar, she doubted she would enact such saving magic. What did she care for the land?

Odjin snarled at the thought. She herself was an orphan, and had been raised as a ward of Kendar's court. She could not understand the humble pleasures of family life, and she despised the peasants and their simple ways.

It was of little consequence, Odjin mused. Soon there would be nothing left of Kendar, and she would have to consider finding a new domain. Already her goblin hordes were crossing the borders and invading the territories of other nations. They returned with rich plunders: chests of gold, silver, and other treasures. Frantic, whimpering ambassadors had come one by one to her court, pleading for mercy, or thrusting hastily-conceived treaties before her throne. They had all been fools. Why would she negotiate for peace, when she had the power simply to take what she wanted? Their kingdoms would fall to her whim, just as Kendar had.

As Odjin contemplated the night sky, she suddenly saw a shooting star. It reminded her of a time in her youth, when she was still friends with the boy-prince Daron. They had snuck out to the castle walls after their curfew to tell stories and watch the starred sky. Together, they had seen a shooting star.

"You have to make a wish when you see a shooting star," Daron had declared.

"Okay," Odjin had responded. "I wish to be Queen of Kendar."

Daron had furrowed his brow beneath his head of fire-red hair at the remark. "You're not supposed to tell your wish," he had claimed with frustration. "Besides, one day I shall inherit Kendar's throne—if you were to be queen, that would mean you'd have to marry me!"

Odjin remembered just gazing at the boy-prince, not saying a word. After a long pause, she simply said, "Okay."

The witch's thoughts were suddenly interrupted by a knock on the tower door and she turned away from the window.

"Always interruptions," she muttered. "These imbecilic goblins are helpless without me."

She crossed the floor in her flowing robes and yanked open the door to see her goblin servant, Jurm, trembling before her. Jurm was a small, wiry goblin with a long hooked nose. He was an obedient servant, but very irksome because his agility and quickness made him a difficult target when she was in one her tantrums and felt like throwing things.

"Oh great witchy witch," the tiny beast addressed, kneeling before her. "Me so sorry disturb you."

"What is it?" Odjin demanded impatiently.

"We catchy human lurky about castle," Jurm replied. "Jurmy's job to tell Queen about all prisoners."

"Very well," Odjin said. "Bring him before my throne. I will meet you there."

"Yes, my Queeny," the small goblin submitted, and he scurried away on all fours.

Odjin snapped her fingers and three more goblins appeared from the shadows of her chamber to take up the flowing train of her dress as she descended the dark tower to her throne room. By the time she arrived, the prisoner was awaiting her, flanked by two of her goblin thugs. He was chained and sported a black eye from tussling with the castle sentries. Odjin settled into her giant, ornate throne, and there was a long, eerie silence as she inspected the human. He was not much more than a boy, unable as yet to grow a beard. He had sandy blond hair and though thin and

somewhat frail, was not altogether unhandsome.

Finally the witch spoke.

"Few people venture into the castle willingly," she stated. "Surely you know the fate of those brought before me?"

"I submit myself to your mercy," the boy said, lowering his head in reverence to the witch. His tone raised Odjin's interest—no one, other than her goblin slaves, had ever freely bowed to her.

"Go on," Odjin said.

"My name is Droy," the boy declared, lifting his head boldly. "I come from the village of Elford, not far from the castle. For ten generations my family has lived and farmed in this valley. But now the land withers beneath us. The soil is depleted, and the sun is harsh. There has been no rain all summer."

"I do not control the weather," Odjin expressed coolly.

"Think how powerful I might be if I could."

"Still, you are powerful," Droy voiced. "I will be honest with you, my mistress. My village was against me coming before you. They put no trust in you. But whether they like it or not, you are the queen, our leader. I accept this. But now I am desperate, for my people—our people, my queen—are in crisis. We need your help."

Odjin softly stroked her chin, and considered the boy's impassioned plea. "Tell me, young Droy," she said after a moment, "do you love me?"

Droy was startled by the question. "My queen?" he asked.

Odjin rose from her throne and approached the kneeling prisoner.

"Rise," she commanded.

Droy did so, but even at his full height, he was a full head shorter than the witch.

Odjin raised her creamy white hand and caressed Droy's cheek. "Look upon me," she whispered.

Her voice was enchanting; Droy found he could not resist her.

"My queen," he begged. "I only want to save my village."

Odjin noticed a tear roll down his cheek as she held his gaze in her own. "You are a noble boy, Droy," she said with a gentle, perfumed breath upon his face. "You are a worthy subject."

Even as she spoke, the boy began to change, and Odjin was enthralled. She had experienced it countless times— the transformation of a human into a goblin—yet she never bored of the sensation. In fact, it was the very thing that kept her alive. With each new goblin, each stolen soul, she chased away old age. She would live forever.

It was over almost too quickly. Droy crumbled to the floor in a heap of long, disfigured limbs. When he next raised his head, his giant, bloodshot eyes no longer betrayed any glimmer of intelligence.

"Me lives to serve you," he lisped.

"Now you will be known as Drooyl," Odjin announced. Then the witch turned her back on the court and, without even awaiting her goblin servants, exited with long graceful strides, quiet and untouched.

Chapter 14

&9

Strange Lodgings

Corranda awoke slowly, into a strange, unfamiliar darkness. She could not see a thing and had no idea where she might be. She was warm and dry at least, though she could hear water gurgling nearby. There was no bed; she could tell she was resting on some sort of nest built of reeds and plants.

The last thing Corranda remembered was plunging into the river and being hit in the head by a stone. Her head was still throbbing, and she winced with pain as she reached back to touch the giant lump left by the rock.

As her eyes adjusted to the darkness, Corranda began to get a better sense of her surroundings. At first she thought she was inside a cave, but when she reached out to touch the nearest wall, she felt the texture of wood and mud. Then Corranda heard something stir in the darkness, and she realized she was not alone.

"Oh, I see you're awake finally," a strange voice declared. "You've been out since last night!"

To Corranda's relief, it was an animal voice. She tried to sit up and get a better look at the animal, and immediately bumped her head on the low ceiling.

"Easy, Corra," the voice came again. "This lodge wasn't

exactly meant for humans!"

The animal waddled over beside her, its vague form taking shape as it approached. A second animal appeared at the side of the first, and Corranda found herself looking at two large beavers. Each had a broad flat tail and a set of large front teeth. To her amazement, Corranda suddenly realized she was inside a beaver lodge! How she had come to be there she did not know, but she had often wondered what the inside of one would be like. Now that she had the chance to inspect one first hand, she could see that it was firmly built using branches, stones, and river mud. The walls were thick and opaque, allowing little light inside.

"Is Kapoora here?" Corranda asked.

"Not at the moment," the bigger of the two beavers said. "She went to discover what became of your other friends. Don't worry; I'm sure she'll return shortly."

"And who are you?" Corranda asked. "How did I get here?"

"So many questions!" the second beaver remarked. "Aren't you hungry, child? Here, we have brought in some food from the woods for you."

At the mention of food, Corranda suddenly felt quite hungry. The beavers had placed a large pile of nuts, wild greens, and berries next to her bed and the girl quickly began to devour the meal.

"My name is Wakashai," said the first beaver. "This is my mate, Eyako. I must tell you how lucky you are, Corra, that we were so nearby when that goblin hit you."

"What happened?" Corranda inquired.

"We answered Kapoora's call for help when you went

94

unconscious," Wakashai explained. "We knew you would drown if we couldn't get you out of the water, but at the same time there were goblins hovering about the banks looking to get their filthy claws on you."

"We realized the safest place for you would be inside our lodge," Eyako continued. "We had to drag you all the way here while trying to keep your head above water! You're a heavy load, child, for just two beavers and an otter!"

"How big is this place?" Corranda asked, feeling the low ceiling with her hand.

Wakashai chuckled. "I'm sure it seems tiny to you," the burly beaver said. "But this lodge is actually quite big by beaver standards. In fact, this very chamber was once the great meeting hall for our entire lodge."

"Oh," Corranda said. "There must be many beavers here then."

"No," Eyako murmured. "There are only we two."

"Once many beavers lived on the Uka," Wakashai explained. "But between humans and goblins, we have been nearly hunted to extinction. Now only Eyako and I live in this lodge."

"Do people really hunt beavers?" Corranda asked.

"Of course!" Wakashai cried. "They like to make hats and mittens out of us—and from otters too, like your friend, Kapoora!"

"But I'm a human," Corranda pointed out. "Why would you help me when humans have caused you so much grief?"

"Tales of your kindness have traveled up and down the river system," Wakashai said. "We know you would never harm any animal, even for food."

"You live in harmony with nature, Corra, not against it," Eyako continued. "We can only hope that other humans learn your ways."

Soon afterwards, Kapoora returned to the lodge. She had scavenged an old horse blanket from the abandoned barn, thinking that Corranda could use it for her bed but the otter was just as happy to see her friend up and about.

"I thought I had lost you for a moment there in the river," Kapoora confided to the girl.

"I'm okay now," Corranda assured her friend. "Did you find out anything?"

"I think the goblins have left you for dead," Kapoora informed her. "They think you drowned in the Uka."

"What about Orufoo and Shutakee?" Corranda asked.

"They're in a spot of trouble, that's for sure," the otter said. "The goblins have set up camp not far from here, and they've got Orufoo and Shutakee in cages. It's those same goblins who chased us out of Cobald. They must have tracked us south."

"What do you think the goblins will do with them?" Corranda urged.

This time Wakashai answered the girl. "They'll eat them, of course," the big beaver proclaimed. "That's what goblins always do!"

"Oh no!" Corranda cried. "We can't let that happen!"

"I'm not sure what we can do," Kapoora admitted. "There's twenty or more goblins in that camp!"

"We'll just sneak in after nightfall and rescue them

while the goblins are sleeping," Corranda suggested.

"That won't work," Eyako said. "Goblins are nocturnal creatures; they do most of their sleeping during the day."

"You could always roll around in the mud again," Wakashai suggested jokingly to Corranda. "When we first got you into the lodge, you were so wet and dirty that you hardly looked human!"

"You just gave me a brilliant idea!" Corranda declared suddenly, her face breaking into a broad smile. "Kapoora, give me that old horse blanket! We'll rescue Orufoo and Shutakee yet!"

Chapter 15

❧

Disguise and Trickery

Over in the goblin camp, Orufoo and Shutakee stirred restlessly in their cages. As nightfall descended, the two friends realized that they had endured the entire day without food or water. They had suffered other tortures too, for the goblins visited their cages frequently to poke them with sticks, or spit at them.

In Orufoo's opinion, however, the most aggravating aspect of his imprisonment was his tiny, unforgiving cage. He could barely fit in it. There was no room to stretch his legs, and his snout had to stick out between two bars at one end.

"I think I have a kink in my tail," Orufoo complained.

"We have bigger worries than your tail," Shutakee informed him. Her own cage sat next to Orufoo's, but was large enough for her.

"You should have more sympathy for my tail," Orufoo grumbled. "It's a woeful 'tale', after all."

"Well, at least those gangly goblins haven't beaten the humor out of you yet," Shutakee observed.

"I guess they'll chew it out," Orufoo remarked, gazing across the goblin camp at a giant cauldron which was beginning to boil over their fire. "I have a feeling that stew pot is for us!"

"I can't argue with you on that one," Shutakee admitted. "If we're going to bust out of here, it had better be soon!"

The possibilities for escape, however, seemed limited. Goblins roamed all about the camp, sharpening their weapons, tending to the cooking fire, or just dozing in the brush. They were not intelligent creatures, but there were so many of them that it would be hard to sneak out of the camp without their notice. Of course, Orufoo and Shutakee needed to break out of their cages first, and that was another problem altogether. The cages were held shut by only a simple hasp and bolt device, but this was enough to prevent either the fox or the crow from springing their doors.

"If Kapoora were here, I expect she could make short work of these clasps with her hand-like paws," Orufoo said.

Just then the fox detected an unfamiliar scent in the goblin camp, and with great difficulty, he twisted his head to the other side of his cage so that he could get a better look at the source of the smell.

"What is it?" Shutakee asked.

"There's someone new in camp," Orufoo told her.

Shutakee followed the fox's gaze to see an unfamiliar figure hobble into view.

"That's the strangest goblin I've ever seen," Shutakee observed.

"He smells funny, too," Orufoo voiced.

"All goblins smell funny," Shutakee pointed out.

"I know that," the fox returned. "Still, there's something not quite right about him."

Shutakee had to agree with her friend. The goblin was unusually tall, but was so crippled that it was bent nearly in two. It snorted and grunted loudly, and it walked by leaning heavily on a crude wooden crutch. Its face and misshapen form were disguised by a large, tattered cloak, though the garment did little to mask the creature's disgusting odor.

When the rest of the goblins saw the stranger enter their camp, they instantly raised their weapons in suspicion.

"Who go there?" Lieutenant Meezle, leader of the troop, demanded. It was a dark night, even for a goblin, and Meezle found it difficult to see the stranger's features.

"Me Goup," the new goblin offered in reply. It did not look up when it spoke, but its voice had a very commanding tone. "Me sent here by Odjin herselfy!"

"That's no goblin!" Orufoo yelped excitedly from his cage. "I can understand her words! It's Corra in disguise!"

101

"You're right," Shutakee said. "Why is she speaking so strangely?"

"She must be trying to talk like a goblin," Orufoo guessed. "How did she get herself to smell so bad?"

"I don't know," Shutakee said. "Let's hear what she has to say!"

"You sent here by witchy?" Lieutenant Meezle asked skeptically. "How come for?"

"To see if you catchy that girly yet," Corranda snapped from beneath the veil of the old horse blanket which served as her disguise. "Girly very important to Odjin. She want findy her."

"Me no believes you. Me never see goblin like you!" Meezle declared. He reached out with a scraggly claw to rip back Corranda's hood, but was instantly met with a quick slash of the girl's crutch.

"Do you dares defy witchy?" Corranda yelled. "You wants me go back and say you refuses me?"

Corranda awaited the goblin's reaction with bated

breath. Though her disguise was the best she had been able to assemble with the materials available to her, she knew it would only take her so far in fooling the goblins. If her plan were to succeed, it would have to be now or never.

"Me don't know," Meezle muttered, his voice still leery.

"Fine," Corranda hissed, turning her back on the goblin. "You explainy to Odjin herself why you no talky me!"

"No, no—don't leaves!" Meezle called out. He had his doubts about Goup, but he wasn't about to chance Odjin's wrath. "Me makey mistake. Goup welcome here. Sitty down. Enjoy warm fires and foody food!"

"I have no time for such thingies!" Corranda grunted. "Just show me girly!"

"We no have her," Meezle confessed.

"We thinky she dead," a second goblin named Wrash interjected. "She drowny in river."

"Need proof!" Corranda lisped. "You have nothing me can show Odjin?"

"We got two little beasties," Meezle said. "They girly's pets, but we catchy them."

"Let's takey look," Corranda dictated with as much authority as she could muster.

Meezle and Wrash led her over to the cages where Orufoo and Shutakee were held captive. "We have big feasty tonight," Meezle announced to Corranda. "You eat with us, eat beasty stew!"

"You can't eat them!" Corranda exclaimed with horror. Her entire body began to tremble with fear, but then she remembered her role and quickly found her most intimidating voice. "No eaty beasties!" she ordered.

"What you talky about?" Meezle cried. "Of course we eat!"

"Me sure beasties be yummy yum, but they valuable prisoners," Corranda snorted. "Must take them to witchy."

"But we want eaty them!" Wrash protested with a panicked voice. He himself had been looking forward to eating the fox and crow all day and, even though he had just devoured an entire peach tree the hour before, he felt as if his pangs of hunger would be the end of him.

Corranda could see that the goblin had a frenzied look in his eye, but she quickly dismissed the complaint with a dangerous wave of her crutch. "Witchy's orders come first," she emphasized. "No more argumenties. Now, let me take closer look at beasties."

She brushed aside Meezle and Wrash and stuck her face close to the mesh of Orufoo's cage.

"Corra, you stink!" Orufoo told her. Now that she was so close, the fox could see that Corranda was covered head to foot in thick black mud to help disguise the natural color of her skin.

"Just be alert!" Corranda whispered, so softly that the goblins could not hear her. "I'm going to distract these monsters long enough so that Kapoora can rescue you!"

Before either Orufoo or Shutakee could respond to the girl's surprising announcement, Corranda turned around to face the bewildered Lieutenant Meezle.

"Odjin let us eaty animals," Meezle said indignantly, hoping to change Corranda's mind about dinner.

"These special beasties," Corranda persisted. "Witchy say girly and all friendy friends must be brought to her directly. If you want, you eaty animals. Then me rip out your tummy tum tum and take it to Odjin."

"No, that okey dokey," Meezle whimpered.

"Very well then," Corranda said, shuffling back towards the fire. "Me go with you rest of journey. Goup in command of troop now."

"Yes sir," the newly-demoted Meezle mumbled. He did not like this affair at all, but Corranda had asserted her authority well, and now Wrash and the rest of the goblins eagerly gathered around the disguised girl in support of her leadership. Corranda let out a sigh of relief.

So far so good, she thought.

Chapter 16

ॐ

The Goblin Camp

T he goblins had not seen Odjin in a long time and were eager to get as much news as possible about the beautiful sorceress.

"You sees Odjin recently?" Wrash asked the girl excitedly. "Me loves witchy, but me no see her in months and months."

"Yes, me sees her short time ago," Corranda replied. She knew she would have to think quickly to respond to the goblins' questions. She had never seen Odjin, of course, nor had she ever been to the castle of Kendar. She could only rely on her imagination to maintain her deception.

"She still purty as ever?" a goblin named Retch asked.

"Of coursey," Corranda scowled. "You dares question witchy's beauty?"

"No, no," Retch said quickly. "Just been so long since me sees her. Other goblins so lucky that get livey in castle and see her all the times."

"Yeah, we never get chance for big fat kissy kiss," said another goblin named Blisster.

"Now big fat Captain Wort gonna be Odjin's favorite," Meezle pouted. "Just because he catchy ugly dwarfy."

In spite of herself, Corranda let out a gasp at the mention

of her uncle. She desperately wanted to ask what was so important about her uncle, but she didn't dare risk compromising her identity. At the very least, she had the distinct impression that Captain Wort wasn't very well-liked by the other goblins, and she wondered if she could somehow use the information to her advantage.

"Wort thinky he so smarty smart," Wrash sneered. "'Looky at me'," he mocked. "'Me big fat Worty and Odjin likey me best!'"

"He stupid too," Corranda added, in an attempt to win their favor. "One time me tell him go hunty bear, and he go out in the woods naked!"

Corranda herself thought her joke was quite clever—at least worthy of Orufoo, but the goblins just stared at her blankly.

"You know," Corranda explained. "Goup mean go hunty grizzly bear, but Wort so dumb he think I mean go bare naked!"

The goblins finally understood the joke and broke out in a round of laughter.

"That's a riot," Blisster roared, giving Corranda a hearty slap on the back. "You tell funny jokies!"

"You telly us more!" Retch pleaded.

Corranda looked about and quickly realized that she had the attention of the entire camp. The goblins were starved for amusement, and she knew if she could entertain them for even a few moments, then Kapoora would have ample opportunity to rescue Orufoo and Shutakee.

"Me do better than jokey!" Corranda promised. "Me singy song about Captain Wort!"

107

A chorus of cheers went up from the goblin soldiers and they formed a semicircle around the disguised girl, eager to hear more insulting remarks about their hated captain.

Just before she started her song, Corranda glanced across the camp and spied Kapoora creeping out of the shadows, towards the cages where her friends were held captive. Everything seemed to be going according to plan.

Then Corranda cleared her throat and began her song, a ballad so crude and disgusting that it was worthy of any goblin:

"Oh, no one so mean as Captain Wort!
When he shouty commands, he lisp and snort!
He like big fatty pimple urging for explosion,
A giant scaly rash that itchies for lotion!
His soul brims over with spite (or so me told),
Seething with bile, ulcers, and belly button mold!
And his hearty heart beats with glass and rusty nails;
A wretched bowl of blisters, boils, and all that ails!"

"That's him all right!" Retch giggled.
"Shush!" Meezle hissed. "Don't wrecky song!"
Corranda continued:

"Oh, no one so vile as Captain Wort;
He make himself vomit, just for sport!
Out of his ears long hairy hair grows,
And with long bony claws he picky his nose!
He give big grin through drool and slime;
His teeth all covered with dirt and fingernail grime!

108

Yes indeed, of all goblins, he most smelly;
His breath reek of booger, pus, and toe-gunk jelly!"

The goblins were now laughing so hard that they were rolling on the ground, grasping their hair-covered bellies.

As Corranda was engaged in her performance, Kapoora worked to free Orufoo and Shutakee from their cages.

"It's about time you showed up!" Orufoo yipped.

"Just keep it down," Kapoora warned the fox as she tugged at the hasp and bolt with her dexterous paws.

"You 'otter' talk," Orufoo returned. "You haven't been locked up all day."

"This is no time for jokes," Kapoora uttered.

With a quiet click, Kapoora pulled back the locking mechanism on Orufoo's cage and the fox crawled onto the grass, painfully stretching his legs.

"Oooh, that's better," Orufoo declared.

Kapoora turned her attention to Shutakee's cage. In the background, they could still hear Corranda's song:

"Oh, no one so greedy as Captain Wort;
He devour every morsel in Queen Witchy's court!
His favorite dish is scabs and toenail toss;
But he also like ear wax roast and green phlegm sauce!
He eat sewery soup with big fatty fat slurp,
And when he done, he let out a gummy burp!
He steal treaty treats, even from babies;
Me see him share only once; he give a dog rabies!"

"Where did she learn to be so disgusting?" Orufoo whispered to his companions.

"She has quite an imagination, all right," Shutakee said. Once the crow was free of her cage, the three friends crept through the grass towards the river.

"What's the plan?" Orufoo asked Kapoora. He was walking very gingerly, trying to get the cramps out of his legs.

"We've built a raft," the whiskery otter replied. "We're to meet Corra at the riverbank, and then we'll float down the Uka."

"How's Corra going to sneak away from those goblins?" Shutakee asked.

"I'm not sure," Kapoora admitted. "We're kind of making this up as we go! All we have to worry about is meeting her at the raft."

Corranda watched her three friends disappear into the darkness and breathed a sigh of relief between verses. Her friends had escaped and now all she had to do was bide her

time until she could slip away from the goblin troop
unnoticed. Then, as she turned to finish the final verse of
her unkindly tribute to Captain Wort, Corranda accidentally
stepped on the corner of her cloak. The blanket caught beneath her heel and, before she knew it, she found herself
standing amidst the entire goblin camp, unveiled!

Meezle and the rest of the goblins stared at her with
giant, gaping mouths, so stunned that they hardly knew
what to do! Only moments before they had been enjoying
the most disgusting song they had ever heard, now only to
discover that its vocalist was nothing more than a wretched,
mud covered human—the very human Captain Wort had

charged them with capturing!

"You no Goup!" Wrash accused. "You girly girl!"

"I knew it!" Meezle declared proudly. "Me know something wrong with Goup!"

"Never mind that!" Blisster shouted. "Let's get her!"

With a roar, the goblins unsheathed their weapons and rushed Corranda, who quickly turned and bolted into the dark woods.

"Don't let her getty away!" Meezle screamed. He was angry at himself for getting fooled by Corranda, and especially for enjoying her song.

The woods were dark and Corranda struggled to scramble over the tangled roots and brush that blocked her path. She knew it wasn't far to the river, but she could hear the goblins thrashing madly through the wilderness, hot on her heels.

Suddenly the icy grip of a goblin's claw encircled her ankle and with a scream Corranda toppled to the ground. She looked back to see the grotesque figure of Wrash standing over her.

"Me got you now, girly!" Wrash hissed and with a smack of his lips, he sank his sharp, jagged teeth into her ankle.

Corranda screamed with pain. The only thing she could think of was to get the goblin off of her. She kicked violently with her free leg and was finally able to plant a foot in Wrash's face, sending the pungent pest rolling into a nearby thorn bush. Corranda's ankle throbbed in agony, but she knew she couldn't pause and examine the wound. Her cry had alerted the entire goblin troop to her exact location; she would have to keep moving. She tried to stand up, but the pain in her ankle was so great that she crumpled to the ground. She could hear Wrash howling, for the hapless goblin could not wrestle free of the thorn bush, and the more he struggled, the more the plant's sharp briars stung him.

"If me get claws on you again, me beaty you good, girly!" Wrash threatened.

Corranda didn't doubt him. She bellied her way over the ground like a snake, trying to get as far away as possible from Wrash. She realized she would never make it to the river before the goblins caught up to her. She needed a hiding place, and she needed it quickly. Then, as she crawled through the underbrush, Corranda came upon a large tree with a great split at the base of its trunk. With a deep breath she squeezed through the crack and into the tree. Too late did she realize that the hollow gave way to a giant underground cavern. She found herself rolling head over heels down a steep decline and landing with a thud at the bottom of the dark underground cave.

Then Corranda became aware of a loud, droning noise. At first she thought it was just the ringing of her ears from her fall, but then she realized what she was hearing was actually the sound of voices, so many that she could not pick out any words. She could not tell if they belonged to friend or foe, only that they were not human. The noise was so intense that it filled the cave with a loud hum. In desperation, Corranda cupped her hands over her ears.

Finally the noise began to subside and the voices united to issue a single, clear demand: "Who dare enters Embo, the realm of the mighty Queen Ixximo?"

Chapter 17

ॐ

The Return of Rollick

The journey south to the castle of Kendar was a long one for Rollick and his gang of captors. The old dwarf did his best to check on Jumba along the way, but the cow was kept near the back of the procession, and Rollick did not have much freedom of movement. At first he worried that the goblins might eat her, but he relaxed his fears when he realized that the gruesome creatures where content to keep the cow alive for her rich, creamy milk.

Wort was eager to get his prisoner to Odjin as quickly as possible, and he pressed the caravan to travel hard and fast. He did not even let his thugs pause long enough to loot or pillage along the way.

"Sooner we get to Odjin, sooner me get reward for finding you, little dwarfy," Wort told Rollick.

"I'm not as important as you think," Rollick claimed.

"Oh, you important," Wort declared. "Witchy going to be very happy see you. Maybe she gives me big fat kissy kiss!"

After four weeks of hard travel, the small band of goblins and their small prisoner reached the south of Kendar, where Odjin's castle stood dark and foreboding in the delta valley of the Uka River.

It was the first time Rollick had been to the valley in more than fifteen years, and nothing could have prepared him for the shock that awaited him. The entire region was besieged by drought. The Uka River, once swift and deep, had been reduced to a stagnant crawl as it slowly wound its way towards the sea. Its waters no longer sparkled blue and clear as Rollick remembered, but were dark and muddy.

The fertile farms that had embraced the banks of the once-mighty river had earned no better a fate, their rich loamy soils having eroded into long plains of dry, gray dust. The crops that had managed to sprout on the exhausted soil were brown and meager, their nutrients bleached out by the harsh and unforgiving sun. There were few farm animals, and those that Rollick did see were scrawny and sickly, with haggard, flea-bitten coats.

The valley had once been home to a large, prosperous population, but now the villages and homesteads lay in ruin. Rollick could see that the houses, barns, and windmills sagged with disrepair.

Most of the windows were broken or boarded up, while giant gaping holes in the walls and roofs revealed gutted interiors. As the goblin caravan passed through the forlorn streets, Rollick witnessed the somber, hopeless expressions that conveyed the people's tales of woe. The old dwarf had known these people when they were strong and vibrant, but he could see that living in such close proximity to the witch and her cruel minions had taken its toll on them, leaving them dull and listless.

As bad as all these things were, nothing was so distressing to Rollick as the state of the castle of Kendar. In Rollick's day, the castle had been a towering feat of pristine architecture, with sculpted buttresses and magnificent spires that yearned towards the skies. Now it seemed nothing more than a blackened mass of rubble. Part of the castle had been destroyed during Odjin's attack fifteen years earlier; many of the towers still lay in ruin, and those that had been repaired were examples of the crudest workmanship. Some new additions had been made to the castle, but these were mostly ugly black turrets and bridges that jutted out from the main palace like giant, ungainly wings.

As Wort led Rollick across the long bridge that connected the island citadel with the mainland, the saddened dwarf got an even closer inspection of the decaying castle. Broken or beheaded statues seemed to cry out from niches in the rampart walls, while ragged tapestries and banners waved forlornly in the wind. Years of grime and soot were caked upon the walls, turning the stones black.

As he was dragged before the powerful witch, Rollick saw that the throne room was the only exception to the castle's ugliness. Thick velvet curtains greeted visitors at the entrance archways, and the floors were laid with giant marble tiles. The chamber was pure and immaculate, the walls and furniture gleaming with recent polishing. Still, there was little decoration in the grand throne room, no statues, tapestries, or plants to fill the hall with life. There were only mirrors—row upon row of shimmering, reflective glass that lined the walls on each side of the witch's great throne, enabling the vain sorceress to contemplate her beauty from every direction.

To Rollick's astonishment, Odjin herself had not changed since the last time he had seen her, that fateful day so many years ago when she had come to King Daron's court. While Rollick's own hair had long turned gray, Odjin had not seemed to age a single day. Her hair was still golden and glorious, her lips still red and luscious. Not a wrinkle lined her pale, beautiful face.

"I see your black arts continue to serve you well," Rollick declared as he was forced to kneel before the witch. "Your beauty is constant, if not petrified."

"Silence, dwarf!" Odjin hissed. "You will not speak unless addressed."

To emphasize her point, she made a subtle gesture to one of her goblin guards, who immediately scurried forward and jabbed Rollick with a broken spear. Rollick grimaced with pain, but held his tongue.

"Very good," Odjin murmured coolly before turning to her captain. "Now, Wort, tell me of your visits to the north. It seems for once you have not returned empty-handed."

"Me bringy back many treasures," Wort announced.

"Yes, I see," Odjin said, reaching down to take a peeled grape from one of her servants. She savored the succulent fruit slowly with her full, delicate lips.

"Me got money and jewels," Wort announced, then paused to scratch his bumpy head as he tried to recount his booty.

"Yes," Odjin prompted.

"Oh, and horsies and piggies," Wort remembered. "We even getty cow that give creamy yummy milk!"

"Of course," Odjin said, her voice growing impatient. "Cows can be good for milk."

"Yes," Wort continued. "We also get some nice chairy chairs and benches . . . oh, we burny most of those to make nice fires though. We have some tools and some food too. I guess that all."

"That's all?" Odjin hissed.

Wort paused for a moment, deep in thought. "Oh, we getty one more thing!"

"Good," Odjin said, leaning over to take another grape. "And what might that be?"

"Wine," Wort replied, very pleased with his memory. "Big vatty of wine, slurpy down really good."

"You idiot!" Odjin screamed, hurling one of her heavy metallic bracelets at the bewildered goblin and nailing him in the head. "The dwarf! Tell me about the dwarf! Isn't that the whole reason you stormed in here without so much as taking a bath, you filthy worm-bitten mongrel!?"

"Oh, yeah yeah," Wort said, rubbing the giant lump that was beginning to form on his forehead. "Me forgety about dwarfy. But me find him good. Me think he little dwarfy that hides princess."

Odjin regarded the dwarf closely. She had known Rollick vaguely, many years ago, but had paid little attention to him then. She could not be sure if this dwarf was indeed Rollick, the same man who had once been one of King Daron's most trustworthy advisors.

"Tell me, what makes you think this is the right dwarf?" Odjin asked her captain. One of her goblins had scurried over to collect her bracelet from the corner of the room and she slipped it back onto her slender wrist.

"Well, he seem to knowy little girly in village," Wort explained. "Let's see...girly about right age. She purty too." Incensed with rage, Odjin peeled off both bracelets this time and flung them at the portly goblin, hitting him squarely in the head in quick succession. "Why do I care if she's pretty or not?" the sorceress yelled furiously. "Is she more beautiful than I?"

"No, no, coursey not!" Wort whimpered. "No one more purty than you, oh great Odjin!"

"Of course not!" Odjin snapped. "But was she the princess? Did she have the mark of the crown upon her neck?"

"Me no know," Wort confessed timidly. "She get away before me looky."

"You let a measly little girl escape you?" Odjin flared.

"She quick!" Wort defended. "She hide in woods like little bunny. Me leave goblins up there to finds her, but me no think they get her yet."

"This is intolerable!" Odjin fumed. She glared down at Rollick, who through all this time had tried to conceal his emotions and fears regarding Corranda. "You dwarf!" the witch called. "What torture must I enact upon you in order for you to tell me the whereabouts of the princess?"

Rollick stared at the marbled floor and did not respond.

"How wearisome," Odjin sighed, picking up another grape and fondling it in her fingers. After a moment's contemplation, she crushed it with a sudden twitch, turning it into a pulpy mass that dribbled slowly down her hand in streams of red juice. "I suppose I could turn you into a goblin," she informed the dwarf. "This would certainly ensure your loyalty. Then you would have no choice other than to tell me everything you know about that wretched girl."

Rollick jerked his head up and looked at the witch, but was careful not to gaze directly into her pale blue eyes. "Do with me as you wish," he proclaimed. "I can tell you no more than you already know. The girl knows those woods like the back of her hand. You can search for her in those tangled wilds the rest of your life for all I care. You'll not find her."

Odjin leaned forward and stared hard at the small man. Despite himself, Rollick started to tremble.

"My dear, stunted little stump of a man," Odjin snarled. "So confident of your ability to hide her from me, are you? Such a clever little man! So clever that you have just given me the most wondrous, splendid idea!"

Rollick's brow furrowed with concern. He could see that the witch was hatching a devious thought, and it worried him.

"Wort, take this pathetic creature from my sight!" Odjin ordered with a dismissive wave of her hand.

"What!" Wort cried. "You no turn him into goblin?" The captain was stunned, for he had never seen Odjin miss an opportunity to disfigure a prisoner with her beauty.

"I have other plans for him," Odjin explained. "We must have a dungeon somewhere in this wreck! Use it!"

With a sigh of disappointment, Captain Wort carted off the hapless dwarf and Odjin was left to brood over the missing princess. *It's plain to see that the dwarf is deeply protective of the girl,* the witch mused to herself. *If she loves that little runt half as much as he loves her, then I hardly think she'll waste her time scampering around in the woods trying to evade Wort's idiotic soldiers. No . . . she'll do everything in her power to rescue the pitiful old man. If she truly is Daron's daughter, then she's surely cursed with his same pathetic sense of honor and loyalty.*

The witch pursed her lips as she savored the thought, then slowly broke into a wide, wicked smile. *I don't have to worry about hunting her!* Odjin thought. *Her quest to save the dwarf will bring her directly to me! I will issue a proclamation across the land, announcing that I have captured a traitor to the crown—the treacherous dwarf Rollick, who will be executed by the first Autumn moon! As soon as the girl hears the news, she will be compelled to rescue him! Indeed, we will find out soon enough if she is truly the lost princess of Kendar!*

Chapter 18

✖✖

A Sticky Situation

S itting wounded at the bottom of the hollow tree, Corranda was too shocked to muster a reply to the strange voice.

It spoke again: "Who dares to breach the domain of Queen Ixximo?"

Corranda's eyes had not yet adjusted to the darkness of the cavern, and she could not see the owner of the voice that commanded her. Her nostrils were overcome with a strong aroma which, though strange, was somehow familiar to her. Then suddenly she realized that the smell was honey! She lifted her hand and discovered that it was coated in the warm, sticky substance. She had landed smack in the middle of a giant bee colony!

"I promise you, I come in peace," Corranda announced. "My name is Corra, but you may know me by my other name: Korr-an-rah!"

Corranda felt a flutter of air near her cheek and focused her eyes to see a large, striped bumble bee buzzing beside her.

"Korr-an-rah?" the bee asked. "Is this the same Korr-an-rah of legend? She who feeds the sparrows in winter? She who nurses the wounded creatures of the wild?"

"It is I," Corranda confirmed. Her eyes finally became

accustomed to the dark, and she gazed upon the magnificence of the cavern. The cave housed a massive complex of wax honeycombs that clung to the tree's extensive network of roots. Thousands upon thousands of bees hummed about the honeycombs, filling each cell with nectar and pollen, the raw materials which would interact with the insects' own saliva to produce honey. Corranda was in awe. Growing up in the woods, she had encountered many bee nests and hives, but had never dreamed of one so big that she could actually crawl inside!

"Give us proof that you are Korr-an-rah!" the bee next to Corranda's face persisted.

Corranda knew of only one way to satisfy his question: she lifted her pipe to her lips and filled the hive with music. Almost at once she could feel the entire colony relax, and

the roaring sound of their wings waned to a quiet hum.

"I beg your pardon," the bee told Corranda. "You are certainly who you claim to be. I am Uzzapo, drone to Queen Ixximo. You are welcome here, Korr-an-rah."

"Thank you," the girl told Uzzapo. "What did you call this place?"

"This is the domain of Embo," Uzzapo replied. "It is the largest hive in all the land. Though our numbers have dwindled severely in the last few years, we are still a mighty colony."

"I believe it," Corranda said, still in awe at the giant underground complex.

"Are you hurt?" Uzzapo asked, noticing the girl's ankle.

"Yes," Corranda confirmed. "I don't think I can climb out of the cave and, even if I could, there's an entire troop of goblins waiting for me!"

"Goblins!" Uzzapo cried.

"Yes," Corranda said. "They're after me."

"Do not fret," Uzzapo consoled the girl. "I will take you before Queen Ixximo herself. She will decide what is best to do. Are you able to make it? The way is not far."

"I'll have to crawl," Corranda said, "but I think I can manage."

Uzzapo fluttered away and Corranda followed after him on all fours. She thought she might lose the feisty bee amidst the rest of the hive, but the other drones parted to make her way clear. She soon found herself in the core of the honeycomb hive, where hundreds more bees buzzed about in dedicated protection of their queen.

"Wait here a moment," Uzzapo informed Corranda. He

disappeared into one of the thousands of honeycomb cells. He seemed to know exactly where he was going, though Corranda wondered how he could be so sure.

After a few moments, Corranda heard Uzzapo's voice again. "Make way for Ixximo, mighty queen of Embo!" the bee proclaimed.

From the center of the largest honeycomb in the cave, Queen Ixximo emerged. Corranda had never seen a bee so big as the queen. She was nearly the size of Corranda's hand, and had a bright golden coat laced with furry black stripes. She had two large eyes that twitched inquisitively and though her translucent wings fluttered constantly, the giant bee moved with a slow and deliberate purpose. The queen regarded Corranda critically for a few moments, then buzzed over to land on the girl's waiting palm.

"So, you are Korr-an-rah," the queen intoned. "Many

tales have I heard of the human who does not harm even a bumble bee. Yet I never thought I would have the honor to meet you!"

"It is a pleasure to meet you too," Corranda said.

"Whatever help you need, we shall give it to you," Queen Ixximo declared.

"Thank you," Corranda said. "I need to get to the riverbank where my friends are waiting."

"There is another way out of the hive," Queen Ixximo told Corranda. "It is not too far, and the entrance opens near the river. We shall take you to this tunnel."

Queen Ixximo made a subtle vibration with her wings and suddenly thousands of bees ushered forth from the honeycombs to whiz about Corranda's body. Before she even realized what was happening, Corranda felt her body rise magically into the air. The bees were transporting her! Corranda could feel the tingle of each bee as it worked to lift her weight, which, to a bee, must have been immense indeed. Slowly, but steadily, Corranda floated through the cave to the roar of the hive's humming labor.

Then suddenly, a loud, distant crash echoed through the colony from the higher levels of the cave. The hive instantly erupted into frenzy.

"The hive has been breached!" Uzzapo cried.

"Hurry!" Queen Ixximo ordered the bees who where carrying Corranda. "Get her out of here!"

Even as she spoke, the regal queen turned and whisked away through the cavern.

High above at the surface, Lieutenant Meezle and the rest of his gangly crew were thumping away with their

128

swords and clubs at the entrance to Embo.

"Girly went in there," Wrash said. He had finally extracted himself from the thorn bush and was eager to get his revenge on Corranda.

Meezle poked his head into the tree's crevice. "It too darky dark in here," he shouted back to his troop. "Someone getty me torch!"

Then Meezle heard a sound and he cocked his head so that he might hear it clearer. The sound was quiet at first, like a soft humming, then began to grow louder and louder, until it reached an immense roar. In a panic, Meezle jerked back and banged his head on the inside of the hollow tree. "Ouch!" the miserable creature howled. "Get me outta here! Quicky!"

Wrash and Blisster each grabbed hold of a leg and began tugging on their lieutenant. Meezle's giant head, however, was now firmly lodged in the tree and pull as they might, the two goblin ruffians could not free him.

"Pully harder!" Meezle ordered frantically.

It was too late; in the next moment the wretched goblin lieutenant was engulfed by a wave of Queen Ixximo's drones and he yelped with pain as the bees embedded their stingers in his scraggly face. Wailing and flailing, the besieged beast finally yanked his head out of the tree, only to release the swarm of bees upon his unsuspecting soldiers!

"Attack!" Uzzapo yelled, leading the charge.

The goblins did not need to be told to run. They scattered through the forest in a vain attempt to escape the angered hive, but the bees seemed to be at every turn, inflicting their painful stingers upon the troops.

Corranda could hear the goblins' squeals through the trees as her magic carpet of bees lifted her out of the cave and down to the shores of the river. There, on the rocky bank, her friends awaited her: Kapoora, Orufoo, Shutakee, and the two beavers. A small raft was floating at the edge of the water, held in place by Wakashai and Eyako.

"Corra, what is going on!?" Kapoora cried, her eyes as wide as saucers.

"I met some new friends!" Corranda declared as the bees lowered her gently onto the raft.

"Go in peace, Korr-an-rah!" the bees buzzed in concert.

"Thank you," the girl called in reply. In the next instant the swarm disappeared, returning to the realm of Embo through the rocky opening in the riverbank.

"You've had a strange adventure, child!" Eyako uttered. "And it appears you've been hurt too!"

Corranda nodded. With her magical ride on the bed of

bees, she had temporarily forgotten her wound, but now the surging pain in her ankle was so great that she could not ignore it. "One of those fiends bit me," she said.

"C'mon," Orufoo urged, scrambling onto the raft alongside the girl. "This has been a strange night. I'm all for leaving this place behind!"

"Good idea," Shutakee said, and she and Kapoora climbed onto the small river craft.

"I guess this is good-bye," Wakashai said.

"Will you come with us?" Corranda asked the two beavers.

"We're not much for high adventure, Corra," Eyako told her. "We have stayed in our lodge through thick and thin. It's where we belong."

"I understand," Corranda said, though she was sad to leave her two new friends behind. "I hope to see you again."

"You can travel much quicker by river," Wakashai said, giving the raft a mighty heave to set it on its way. "You'll have to watch for goblins of course, but one thing's for sure: this particular bunch shouldn't bother you again!"

"Good-bye!" Eyako called, as the raft floated down the river.

"Good-bye!" Corranda shouted in reply. She watched the two beavers bobbing in the moonlit water, then the raft turned a bend in the river, and she saw them no more.

Chapter 19

❧

A Tough Decision

A day later, Orufoo was still trying to get over what he had seen by the riverbank. It was all he could talk about.

"Those bees carried Corra all by themselves," he yipped as they floated down the river in the warm, late summer sun. "I don't know who I'll be able to tell. No one would bee-lieve me. Get it—'bee'-lieve!"

"It's a good thing those goblins didn't eat you, for their sake," Shutakee told the fox. "Your poor humor may have given them a bad stomachache!"

"Stop bickering!" Kapoora scolded. "Corra's trying to sleep!"

At the mention of Corranda, the fox and the crow instantly ceased their chatter and looked over at their friend, who was stretched out on the raft in a fitful sleep. Kapoora had diligently washed and bound the girl's ankle the day before, but the wound had since turned purple and yellow with infection. Corranda now had a dreadful fever and was muttering incoherently in her sleep.

"She's not getting any better," Orufoo observed. "It's those wretched goblins. Their saliva is so full of bacteria, it's no wonder Corra is ill."

"I don't like this situation," Shutakee fretted. "We need to get Corra off the river. Maybe we should camp in the woods for a few days until her fever breaks."

"We need to do more than that," Kapoora told them. "Corra is really sick. She needs help from her own kind. Human help."

"Humans!" Orufoo cried. "I'm not going to trust Corra to a bunch of humans! Who knows what they'll do to her? If nothing else, they might corrupt her. They might make her more like them!"

"They might save her, too," Kapoora argued. Just then the raft hit a patch of rough water and the disturbance caused Corranda to moan and fidget uneasily.

"I don't know if we have much choice," Shutakee declared. "I don't trust humans any more than you do, Orufoo, but I don't see why they wouldn't help Corra. She's one of them, after all."

"Barely," Orufoo muttered. "She's not much like any human I've ever known."

"This arguing is point-less," Kapoora said. "Are we in agree-ment or not?"

"Okay, okay," Orufoo said. "We must find Corra some help."

"Good," Kapoora said. "I'm not sure what's around here, but we need to locate a farm or something nearby."

"I'll see what I can find," Shutakee cawed, stretching her black wings.

The crow took to the air and was soon gone from sight. After an hour or so, she reappeared and lit on the raft.

"Any luck?" Kapoora asked.

"There's not much around here," Shutakee informed her friends. "It looks like goblins have been through here not so long ago, because most of the farms have been destroyed or abandoned. It's the same for some distance down the river."

"What are we going to do?" Orufoo asked. He was beginning to show signs of worry, something quite unusual for the otherwise carefree fox.

"I did find one small farm that hasn't been abandoned," Shutakee said reluctantly to her friends.

"Well, let's take Corra there" Kapoora said.

"There's only one small problem," Shutakee confided.

"Well, what's that?" Kapoora asked.

"I couldn't see any adults there," the crow replied. "Just human cubs!"

"Children!" Orufoo exclaimed. "What happened to their parents?"

"How should I know?" Shutakee said. "But I can tell you this—they're the only humans around here!"

"How close are these human cubs?" Kapoora asked.

"With the speed we're making on this raft, we should reach them before sundown," Shutakee said.

"Okay," Kapoora said after a moment's deliberation. "I don't see how we have any choice. I say we get these children to help Corra."

"They might be too young to help," Orufoo argued.

"They must be capable enough if they live on their own," Kapoora pointed out.

"Anything will be better for Corra than staying on this river," Shutakee said.

"All right," Orufoo grudgingly accepted. "If it's the best for Corra, then I agree."

The issue was settled. As the raft approached the farm, Kapoora and Orufoo dived into the river and pushed the crude wooden craft ashore. The raft bumped hard into the bank, but Corranda was so consumed with fever that she was oblivious to the whole affair.

"How far is it to the house, Shutakee?" Kapoora asked as she and Orufoo climbed out of the swirling waters of the river to rest on the shore next to the raft.

"It's just over the bank," the crow said. "Of course, that's farther than we'll be able to carry Corra. We'll have to get those children down here to find her somehow."

"You can leave that to me," Orufoo announced, shaking the water briskly from his fur. "You two hide. I'll have those human pups down here before you know it."

With that, the rusty-colored fox slipped through the hedges that trimmed the riverbank, leaving behind a muddy set of paw prints.

"I hope he knows what he's doing," Kapoora uttered.

"He never knows what he's doing," Shutakee reminded the otter. "Still, it never seems to stop him!"

It didn't take long for Orufoo to track down the whereabouts of the children with his trusty nose. There were two of them, a boy and a girl, and he found them in a dusty field behind the farmhouse, picking out small, stunted cobs of corn for their dinner. To Orufoo the corn didn't seem like it would make much of a meal, but the land was so blighted that he supposed the children were lucky to have anything to eat at all. Their clothes were old and ragged, and they had no shoes or stockings. Their hair was long and tangled, looking as if it hadn't been cut in months.

Hidden from view by the tangle of brown weeds that choked the edge of the cornfield, Orufoo watched the two children with curiosity. He knew human cubs usually didn't survive on their own at so young an age, and he had a hard time believing there were no adults about. Just to be sure, he gave the air a good long sniff.

Shutakee's right, I suppose, the fox told himself after a few moments. *I don't smell any other humans around here. These pups must be here by themselves!*

As Orufoo was watching, the boy stopped to rest on a nearby tree stump. The child was wearing an old, tattered cap, but let it drop to the ground while he wiped the sweat from his young brow. Orufoo knew he would never have a better chance to get the boy's attention and he dashed into the field to snatch up the cap. The wily fox paused only long enough so that the children could see his direction, then tore off through the bushes towards the river, the cap clenched tightly in his teeth.

"Come back here, you thief!" the boy yelled, shaking his fist. He leaped up and raced after the fox. The young girl was hot on his heels.

"Finn, you leave that critter alone!" the girl yelled. "He

136

might bite you!"

"Then I'll bite him back!" Finn hollered over his shoulder. "That's the only hat I got!"

Finn and the girl wrestled their way through the withered hedge and stumbled down to the river, where they had seen the fox escape. It didn't take them long to find the hat; Orufoo had strategically set it on the raft next to Corranda's motionless body.

"Finn, where did she come from?" the girl exclaimed at the sight of Corranda. It had been a long time since the

children had seen another human, and they almost couldn't believe their eyes.

"I have no idea," Finn said. "You wait here, Kess. I'll go take a closer look." Barefoot, the boy picked his way across the graveled shore. Cautiously he approached the raft. It only took a glance at Corranda's pale, sweat-covered face for the boy to realize she was in serious jeopardy. He touched her forehead to confirm her fever.

"Kess, this girl's real sick! She's burning up!" Finn called. "Come help me! We need to get her up to the house."

Kess didn't hesitate to follow Finn's orders; she was eager to get a closer look at the stranger.

"C'mon," Finn said. "Help me pick her up."

Each child took one side of Corranda's frail body and lifted her from the raft. The children were surprisingly strong for their size and age and without too much difficulty, managed to drag Corranda up the bank. Corranda mumbled and moaned the entire time, but Finn and Kess soon had her inside their house.

The children were so engrossed with Corranda's mysterious appearance that they completely forgot about the strange fox who had led them to the girl. They did not see the crafty animal hiding in the bushes that lined the river, watching with his two friends.

"Well," Orufoo said to Kapoora and Shutakee, "do you think we did the right thing?"

"I sure hope so," Kapoora replied.

Chapter 20

❧

Help and Hospitality

T he first things Corranda saw when she awoke two days later were Kess's warm brown eyes staring into her own. The small girl held a bowl of cool river water and was dabbing Corranda's forehead with a cloth.

"I think your fever's finally broke," Kess declared.

"Fever?" Corranda murmured in confusion. It took her a few moments to realize she was in a human dwelling. After her previous adventures with Wakashai, Eyako, and Queen Ixximo, it was strange to find herself in a real bed, with real sheets and covers. "What happened?" Corranda asked, trying to sit up.

"Finn and I found you by the river, lying on a raft," Kess replied, setting down the bowl and cloth. "Finn is my

brother. He'll be in soon. He's out working in the field."

"And what's your name?" Corranda asked.

"I'm Kess," the girl replied.

"Nice to meet you, Kess," Corranda said. "You can call me Corra."

"That's a pretty name," Kess commented.

"Thank you," Corranda said, looking about her in an attempt to get a better sense of her surroundings. The house seemed to consist of only one room, and an empty one at that. Other than the bed, the room contained only two chairs, a stove, and a few cooking implements. There were only three windows in the whole house, and the doorway was nothing more than an empty frame.

"We aim to get a door on before the bad weather sets in," Kess said in defense of her impoverished home. "We haven't really needed it yet, it being summer and all."

"Whatever happened here?" Corranda asked.

"Goblins attacked us," Kess answered. "They stole most everything we had. What they didn't take, they busted."

Corranda studied the girl with interest. She was small and skinny, with fair blonde hair and a freckled face. She looked no more than ten years old, but Corranda could tell that she knew how to look after herself. "Where's your mother?" Corranda asked.

"Oh," Kess said in reply, "our parents got turned into goblins. I guess we're orphans now."

"That's horrible!" Corranda exclaimed.

"It's all right," Kess said. "Finn and I look after each other now."

"I'm an orphan too," Corranda confided. "I guess I know

how you feel."

Kess looked as if she might cry for a moment, then seemed to catch herself and choked back her tears. "You better not strain yourself too much," Kess said, quickly changing the subject. "You're still pretty weak. What happened to you anyway?"

"I ran into some goblins," Corranda said. "One bit me on the ankle, and I guess he poisoned me!"

"I think you'll be okay now," Kess said. "You just need to regain your strength. I'll heat up some vegetable broth for you—sorry, we don't have any meat."

"That's all right," Corranda told her. "I like animals too much to eat them. Which reminds me, have you seen my friends?"

Just then Finn appear-
ed at the open doorway.
"What friends are those?"
he asked.

Corranda smiled at
the boy as he approach-
ed her bed. "You must be
Finn," she said. The boy
looked to be about twelve
years old and was wear-
ing a pair of old overalls
that were much too big
for him.

"Who are you?" Finn
asked bluntly.

"Her name's Corra,"

141

Kess said. "That wound on her ankle came from a goblin!"

"You're lucky to be alive then," Finn said. "But I don't know what became of your friends. When we found that raft, you were all alone. How many other people were with you?"

"No, not people," Corranda explained. "My friends are animals."

Finn laughed. "That's absurd," he said. "Animals can't be friends! They're animals!"

"You just have to learn to understand them, I guess," Corranda said. "For me, it's not much of a problem. You see, I can talk with animals!"

"You can?" Kess exclaimed.

"She's lying," Finn told his younger sister. "No one can talk to animals."

"I can prove it," Corranda defended. Her pipe was still around her neck; she lifted it to her mouth and played a gentle song that filtered out the window next to her bed. In her weakened condition, it was a labor to blow on the pipe, but in the next few minutes Orufoo appeared at the doorway.

"Corra, you're awake!" the fox barked with excitement, though he eyed the two children suspiciously.

"Don't just stand at the door like that," Corranda told the fox. "It's rude."

"Well, I don't trust these human pups," Orufoo declared. "That boy looks like the kind to carry a sling."

"Don't be ridiculous," Corranda scolded. "Just come over here."

Orufoo warily crossed the hard wooden floor towards

Corranda, but would not take his eyes from Finn and Kess. The children returned his glare with a pair of amazed expressions. They couldn't understand the fox's yips and other canine sounds, but it was clear that he and Corranda were communicating. They watched in bewilderment as Orufoo sauntered right into the middle of their house and jumped up on the bed to lay alongside Corranda.

"Soon as you're ready, we can get out of here," Orufoo said to her.

"I'm in no hurry," Corranda said. "It's nice to sleep in a real bed for once. I think I might stay here for a few days."

"Well, I wouldn't want you to get too accustomed to these pups," Orufoo voiced. "You might forget about your old forest friends."

"That will never happen," Corranda assured the fox, scratching him behind his pair of pointed black ears. "Where are the others, anyway?"

"Shutakee is scouting about the area for goblins, and Kapoora has gone for a swim in the river," Orufoo replied. "We've been taking turns watching you from afar. We left you with these humans because we thought they might help you, but we weren't sure if we were just getting you into more trouble!"

"You don't have to worry about Finn and Kess," Corranda promised the fox. "They're regular people."

"That's what worries me," Orufoo said. "Most people treat animals poorly."

"I refuse to believe that all people are bad," Corranda said. "Finn and Kess certainly aren't!" She looked over at the two children who were standing like two statues, a safe distance from the fox. "Come here," Corranda prompted the children. "Come meet Orufoo!"

"That's the fox that stole my hat," Finn said.

"He's a wild critter," Kess added. "You sure he won't bite us?"

"He won't hurt you," Corranda said. "Don't be afraid!"

"What kind of name is Finn anyway?" Orufoo asked Corranda as the two children approached him. "It sounds kind of fishy to me—you know, fishes have fins!"

"What's he saying?" Finn asked Corranda as he reached out with a nervous hand to touch the fox.

"He's making a joke," Corranda said. "A poor one at that."

"Oh, I was just 'kidding' around," Orufoo retorted in self-defense.

"I had no idea foxes told jokes," Finn said in bewilderment.

"How do you talk to him?" Kess asked Corranda as she petted Orufoo's back. The fox stirred uncomfortably, but after realizing that the boy and girl had no intention of harming him, he settled down.

"It's the magic of my pipe that allows me to communicate with animals," Corranda said. "Birds, fish, animals—I can talk with them all!"

"Well, I'll tell you one thing, Corra," Finn announced. "You're the strangest person I've ever met!"

Chapter 21

ભઈ

Renewed Urgency

Corranda spent the next five days resting and recovering her strength. Kess fed her vegetable broth and tended to her ankle, and Corranda soon found herself improving.

When she was strong enough to get out of bed, Corranda washed and mended her clothing, performed some minor repairs to the raft, and helped Finn and Kess with their chores. The farm had once been prosperous, but the harsh drought and goblin attack had left it in ruin. There once had been a small barn to house the family's chickens, sheep, and pigs, but the goblins had stolen all the animals and trampled the building until there was nothing left of it but a pile of broken boards and rusted nails. The goblins had ransacked the house too, smashing the windows, breaking down the door, and stripping the room of most of its contents.

"I'd like to know how your parents got changed into goblins," Corranda told Finn one morning as she helped the boy weed a small vegetable plot. "Will you tell me?"

"If you like," Finn said, pausing to wipe the sweat from his forehead.

"When did the goblins come?" Corranda asked as she

tugged at a particularly stubborn weed.

"It was two months ago," Finn said. "Kess and I were supposed to be bringing water up from the river for the garden. But it was a hot day, and we decided to climb up that big tree near the house and hide in its shady limbs. We were shirking our chores, but I guess it saved us in the end because when the goblins attacked, they didn't see us. They plundered and wrecked the farm, but didn't even know we were there."

"They're abhorrent creatures," Corranda said. "I'm not sure there's anything worse than goblins."

"There's one thing," Finn said.

"What's that?" Corranda asked.

"The witch," Finn replied solemnly.

"Odjin?" Corranda cried.

Finn nodded. "She was here," he said quietly. "She came

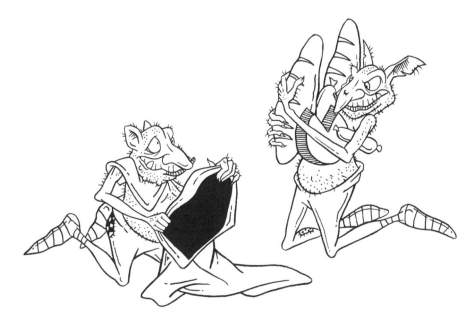

after the goblins, when they were finished destroying every-thing. I had heard all sorts of stories about her, but I never thought I would see her in person. She stays in the castle mostly, but every now and then they say she goes through the land so that she can flaunt her power before the people. They say she loves nothing more than to find new victims."

"Victims?" Corranda asked with puzzlement.

"People to change into goblins," Finn explained. "She does it with her beauty. She forces you to gaze upon her face and—bam—you're transformed into one of those re-pugnant beasts!"

"And she did this to your parents?" Corranda asked, amazed by the boy's tale.

"She turned them into goblins right before our very eyes, while we were hiding in that tree," Finn recounted. "It was quick. One minute they were humans and the next they were goblins. Kess started to cry when she saw them; I had to hold my hand over her mouth so that they wouldn't hear us. Luckily, Odjin and her goblins didn't stick around very long."

"And they took your parents with them," Corranda mur-mured.

"They're not our parents anymore," Finn said. "They're just another pair of goblins, out to ravish the country."

"But why haven't you left this place?" Corranda asked. "Don't you have friends or family to go to?"

"No," Finn said. "This is the only home Kess and I have ever known. I guess we just decided to stay here."

"You and your sister are very brave," Corranda told the boy. "I only hope I can show as much courage."

"What do you mean?" Finn asked.

"My uncle was captured by goblins," Corranda replied. "I'm going to Odjin's castle to rescue him."

"Don't do that!" Finn cried, reaching out and grabbing Corranda's arm. "It's much too dangerous!"

"I have to go," Corranda declared.

"It's a waste of time," Finn argued. "Your uncle has been changed into a goblin by now."

"I don't know that for sure," Corranda remarked.

"I do," Finn implored. "Odjin spares no one! Why don't you stay here, Corra? If you try to save your uncle, you'll just get captured—then you'll be a goblin too. Just stay here, with us."

Corranda stared into Finn's face and considered his offer. Even though she had known Finn and Kess for only a short time, Corranda had formed a strong attachment to them. Her time on the small farm had made her realize how much she craved human affection and friendship, and she knew she would be sad to leave the children behind.

"I would love nothing more than to stay here with you and Kess," Corranda told the boy. "But I have to find my Uncle Rollick. I know it may seem hopeless, but I have to try."

Finn sighed. While there was no doubt in his mind that Corranda's uncle was already a goblin, he could see that the girl would not be deterred from her quest.

"I hope I'm wrong," Finn whispered sincerely.

"Me too," Corranda murmured.

As it turned out, Finn was wrong about Rollick. Early the next morning Shutakee burst into the house with some urgent news.

"Wake up, Corra, wake up!" the bird cried, beating her wings furiously as she fluttered over the sleeping girl.

"Shutakee?" Corranda murmured, as she lifted her head and rubbed the sleep from her eyes. "What's wrong?"

"You better take a look at this," Shutakee stated. In one claw she held a crumpled sheet of parchment which she nudged over to the girl.

"What's this?" Corranda asked, as she flattened out the parchment.

"I'm not sure," Shutakee replied, "but it has a picture of your uncle!"

"Oh no!" Corranda gasped as she gazed upon the contents of the paper.

"What does it say?" Finn asked worriedly.

"It's a royal proclamation from Odjin herself," Corranda replied. "Listen here:

> *By order of the magnificent, mighty,*
> *and illustrious Queen Odjin the Beautiful,*
> *it is hereby declared that this dwarf*
> *shall be executed on the first day*
> *of the autumn moon for crimes and*
> *treacheries committed against*
> *the crown of Kendar!"*

"When is the first autumn moon?" Kess asked.

"It's only a few weeks away," Corranda said. "Shutakee, where did you find this?"

"Hanging on a fence post on the side of the road," the crow answered. "I chanced to see it when I stopped to rest during my morning scouting trip. There are many more of them, scattered all over the countryside."

"This doesn't make any sense," Finn said, scratching the top of his head. "Why would Odjin execute your uncle, Corra? The witch doesn't kill people—she just turns them into goblins!"

"I'm not sure what's going on," Corranda admitted, still in shock from the proclamation. "But, I do have to get to the castle as soon as possible! Shutakee, round up Orufoo and Kapoora. We're leaving right away!"

"We'll be ready in no time," Shutakee declared, taking to the air.

"Corra," Finn said, stepping in front of the girl, "I want to come with you. I want to help rescue your uncle."

"No, it's too dangerous," Corranda argued as she quickly dressed.

"I'm old enough to help!" Finn persisted.

"I don't question your usefulness, or your bravery, Finn," Corranda said. "But I won't take you. Who will stay with Kess?"

"I'll come too!" Kess piped up.

"No, I won't allow it," Corranda said firmly. "Besides, I'm going to travel by the river, and my raft simply won't hold all of us."

"We can build a bigger raft," Kess suggested.

"There's no time," Corranda argued. "My decision is made. Stay here and look after each other. This farm is what is most important for you."

Kess wrapped her small arms around Corranda and sobbed into her bosom. "Oh, don't go, Corra!" the child cried. "I don't want to be without you."

"Everything will be alright," Corranda assured her, stroking the child's head. "After I rescue Uncle Rollick, I'm coming back for you both. You won't be alone anymore."

Understanding that Corranda was determined to go without them, Finn turned his attention to packing some food and other essential supplies for her, despite her objections.

"You have so little," Corranda said. "And you have been so generous already. I don't want to take anything more from you."

"Please accept this gift," Finn responded. "You've done so much for us, Corra, though you may not realize it."

"Thank you," Corranda said, gratefully accepting the package. She hugged the children one last time, then headed out of the house and down to the riverbank where Orufoo, Kapoora, and Shutakee were awaiting her by the raft. Finn and Kess followed after her, doing their best to wipe away their tears as Corranda boarded the small wooden craft.

"Don't forget us!" Kess pleaded as Corranda pushed the raft away from the shore with a long wooden pole.

"I won't!" Corranda promised. "I love you both!"

Finn and Kess sadly watched as Corranda and her animal companions drifted out of sight.

"She left so suddenly," Kess sniffled. "Do you think we'll ever see her again?"

"I don't know," Finn replied. "I just don't know,"

The boy took his sister's hand, then turned and led her quietly back to the farmhouse.

Chapter 22

✿

King of the Uka

*A*s Corranda and her friends traveled down the Uka River, winding their way farther and farther towards the castle of Kendar, they came to witness ever-increasing poverty and despair. The countryside was dry and dusty, its fields bereft of grain or melon, and even the river slowed and became shallower.

"And I thought the rest of the country was poor," Orufoo commented.

"It's as if the land has been poisoned," Kapoora observed.

"How near do you think we are to the castle?" Corranda asked. Her thoughts were consumed with rescuing her uncle, and she was desperate to reach him.

"It can't be much farther," Shutakee offered, dipping her beak over the side of the raft to wet her parched throat. "Try not to worry, Corra; we'll reach your uncle in time."

"I hope so," Corranda murmured.

Finally, after eight days on the Uka, the raft and its small crew floated into the wide valley where Odjin's castle stood high and menacing on its rocky island near the river's exit into the vast Samboora Sea. Even from a distance, the castle's sheer size was foreboding. It stood as a giant in the

river valley, dominating the landscape and cloaking the surrounding farms and villages in its ominous shadows.

"I can't say I'm looking forward to going inside that
thing," Orufoo announced with a grimace. "This whole valley reeks of goblin, and I bet the castle's even worse!"

"We can always leave you behind," Shutakee said.

"That's a fowl suggestion," Orufoo retorted.

"Foul?" Shutakee retorted. "What do you mean by that?"

"Foul—as in it's your cruel suggestion and you are a fowl," Orufoo explained. "It's a pun."

"At least the heat hasn't affected your humor," Kapoora remarked.

As Corranda and her companions drifted towards the castle, they sadly witnessed the poverty of the homes and farms that lined the river. The people appeared skinny and forlorn. Some stared at the raft's strange crew, but otherwise paid them no mind. They had problems of their own to worry about, and could not be concerned with the strange girl who traveled with wild animals.

Corranda and her friends saw goblins, too, but the repugnant creatures showed no interest in leaving the shoreline to capture them.

"I guess those goblins don't know that we're fugitives wanted up north," Orufoo commented.

"Maybe they're just waiting for us to come ashore," Shutakee said. "Then they won't have to get wet. After all, they hate water."

"The only place we're going ashore is at the castle," Corranda said. "Still, I'm not sure how we're going to get inside."

"I doubt Odjin's guards will let us just saunter through the main gates," Kapoora said.

"There has to be another way inside," Corranda mused, scratching her head.

"Perhaps I can be of assistance to you," came a deep, booming voice, so nearby that Corranda jumped with surprise.

"That voice came from the river!" Orufoo yelped.

Corranda leaned over the edge of the raft and stared into the gray, murky water. "Who goes there?" she asked.

"It is I, Ukagee the sturgeon," the voice replied. The water parted and a giant fish poked its head above the surface of the river, next to the raft. The creature was big and black, with a giant lower jaw that had long whiskers. Large bony scales ran down the length of his back and along his sides.

"Where did you come from?" Shutakee asked the great fish. "Were you spying on us?"

The sturgeon let out a mighty bellow. "I don't have to spy on you!" he replied sternly after he was finished laughing. "These are my waters on which you trespass! I am king of the Uka, though Odjin would like to think the river belongs to her. For many years her goblins have tried to catch me with their nets and spears, but I have outsmarted them. So far anyway!" Ukagee laughed again, but after a moment he regarded Corranda with a critical eye. "You are Korr-an-rah," he said. It was more of a statement than a question.

"Yes, I am," Corranda said, somewhat bewildered by the giant creature's strange demeanor. "We did not mean to trespass," she added. "We are only trying to get to the island so that we might enter the castle."

"You and your friends are welcome in my waters," Ukagee declared after a moment's consideration. "Many a water craft have I overturned with my mighty tail so that humans and goblins alike might learn to respect the river. Still, they are such slow learners! But you, Korr-an-rah, come before me with humility and regard. The stories that have been passed down the river about you do you no discredit."

"Thank you," Corranda said. The large fish was somewhat long-winded, but since Corranda was eager to get his help, she decided that the least she could do was to let him talk for a few minutes before enlisting his aid.

"As for the castle, most people seem to use the bridge to get to it," Ukagee said. "Though, come to think of it, few people go there by their own will. It's mostly those gruesome goblins and their human prisoners."

"My uncle is in there," Corranda informed the fish. "We're here to rescue him."

"Ah yes, the dwarf," Ukagee mused, his head glimmering in the light of the setting sun. "I have heard of his forthcoming execution. Well, it is very dangerous to enter Odjin's fortress. I suppose I cannot convince you to abandon your mission?"

Corranda shook her head. "Never," she said.

"Do you know how we can get inside the castle?" Kapoora asked the fish.

"Yes, there are ways," Ukagee replied. He dipped back

157

beneath the water and swam a circle around the raft. He seemed to be thinking the situation through, and after a moment, surfaced again. "I know of a second gate, my friends. It is on the far side of the island, opposite the bridge. Once upon a time it was employed by the king's royal servants, but now the gate has fallen into disrepair like the rest of the castle. The walls will be guarded, but the gate itself is rusted open; if you can avoid being spotted by the goblins, getting inside should be no problem."

"You are a great help," Corranda told the fish gratefully. "Can you lead us to the gate?"

"You mean to go tonight?" Ukagee inquired.

Corranda nodded.

"Very well, Korr-an-rah," Ukagee said. "I will take you to the gate. I wish you would reconsider putting yourself at such risk, but I understand your desire to save your uncle. We must protect what is ours, after all, humans and stur-

geon alike. This is why I will never leave the Uka, no matter
how many stones and spears the goblins hurl down upon me
from the safety of their castle walls. I was born in this river
and will never abandon it to those wretched beasts!"

"How will you take us there?" Orufoo asked, anxious to
interrupt the talkative fish. He had never met anyone who
liked to talk as much as himself and decided that he would
be much happier when Ukagee was gone and he didn't have
to compete with him.

"You must follow me on your raft," Ukagee said. "Throw
me some rope and I will pull you to the island."

Corranda produced a length of twine and the raft was
soon hitched to the mighty Ukagee.

"Here we go," the sturgeon proclaimed, clamping his
giant mouth to the loose end of the rope. "Hang on!"

Corranda and her friends didn't have to be told twice.
As Ukagee tore across the river, the water sprayed up from

the sides of the raft and it was all they could do to not to tumble into the water. Shutakee quickly took to the air, for she did not care for the spray of the muddy water.

"Sometimes I wish I could fly like that crow," Orufoo grumbled, eyeing Shutakee enviously as she soared high above the drench.

Despite how awesome the castle had looked when they had first entered the valley, Corranda realized they were still some distance from the gigantic citadel. For nearly two hours Ukagee pulled them down the river, but by the time he came to a stop at the rocky shores of the island, he was barely out of breath.

"You are incredibly strong," Corranda told Ukagee as she disembarked from the raft. "Are there many more like you on the river?"

"There were many sturgeon back in the days before Odjin became queen," Ukagee replied. "Now I am the only one. Of course, the entire river teemed with life then. Now the Uka is like the rest of the kingdom, a mere shadow of its former self."

"I hope one day we may have happier times," Corranda said. "For me, finding my uncle will be a good start."

"You will see a path up the cliffs which will lead you to the gate you seek," Ukagee told the small band of rescuers.

"Do you know where we might find Corra's uncle?" Kapoora asked Ukagee.

"I have heard from Jamakee the gull that they are holding him in a cell, deep within the castle dungeons," Ukagee revealed. "Of course, I myself have never been inside the keep, but Jamakee tells me that the gate to the dungeon is across from the giant statue of Odjin that stands near the center of the castle."

"Thank you for your kindness, Ukagee," Corranda said, leaning down to pat the fish on its immense head. "You have helped me more than you could ever know."

"You are welcome, Korr-an-rah," Ukagee said. "My thoughts are with you." With that, the enormous fish disappeared beneath the surface of the river and quietly slipped away.

"Well," Corranda whispered, turning to her friends. "I guess we're on our own now!"

Chapter 23

ঞ

The Castle of Kendar

Quietly and carefully, Corranda and her companions climbed up the steep, narrow path that cut its way through the island cliff face towards the gateway. Long before they reached the gate itself they could hear the goblin guards who patrolled the outer walls of the castle, for the churlish beasts had stolen a keg of ale from Odjin's cellars and were now jeering and hurling drunken insults at one another.

Corranda crept as close as she dared to the gate and peered over a large boulder to get a better sense of the situation. The gate was just as Ukagee had described it, rusted open from years of disuse. Corranda counted no less than eight goblin guards staggering about the entranceway, their disfigured silhouettes standing out clearly against the warm glow of the torchlight that emanated from within the castle.

"The gate won't be a problem," Corranda told her friends. "We just need to get past the guards."

"They may be drunk and not too bright, but all it takes is one to sound the alarm," Shutakee cautioned. "What we need is a distraction."

"I think I can manage that," Kapoora whispered. "I'll be

back in a minute; just hang tight!"

The otter slipped back down the path to the riverside and rolled about in the bank until she was covered head to foot in mud.

"Kapoora, what have you done to yourself?" Corranda exclaimed in whispered tones when the otter returned.

"Listen, Corra," Kapoora whispered, "I will distract the guards so that you might pass. Do not wait for me, for you must try and find your uncle as quickly as possible."

"What are you going to do?" Corranda asked.

"Do not worry about me," Kapoora advised. "We will meet again, child."

Kapoora touched her muddy nose to Corranda's cheek, then turned and sauntered directly up to the castle gate where the goblin guards were busily draining the last of their keg.

"That otter's got grit," Orufoo declared. "Actually, she's got it all over her!"

"Shush!" Corranda uttered as she peered over the boulder. "No jokes now, Orufoo!"

Corranda watched with bated breath as Kapoora strode boldly into the midst of the goblins, who were so surprised by the otter's sudden appearance that it took them a moment to gather their wits.

"What beasty beast doing here?" one of the goblins slurred.

"Maybe it sicky sick," a second guard suggested.

The goblins gathered in a circle around the otter, eager for a closer look. Kapoora waited until they closed in about her and then suddenly began to shake her coat, splattering the entire troop with mud, grime, and—worst of all—water!

"Ugh!" the head guard screamed in anger. "Destroy that little pesty pest!"

The goblins immediately raised their spears and crossbows, but before they could notch the first arrow, Kapoora turned and dived off the edge of the rock face and into the swirling river below. The goblins raced to the edge of the bank, desperate for some sign of the troublesome otter.

"There's that wretched beasty!" one of the goblins shouted as Kapoora poked her head out of the water. "Get it!"

Kapoora suddenly found herself besieged by a shower of arrows, spears, and rocks, but she was such a quick and agile swimmer that she easily avoided the goblin assault. She was the fastest of all otters on the Uka River and she knew she was too speedy a target for the drunken guards. She streamed back and forth across the surface of the river with brazen confidence, tempting the goblin guards to hit her, but the more they fired, the more they missed, and the more they missed, the more angry they became.

"Now's our chance!" Shutakee whispered to Corranda and Orufoo. "Let's go!"

The crow streaked towards the gate with the fox and the girl close behind her. The goblins were so eager to attack Kapoora that they did not even notice the small band of rescuers sneaking behind their backs and into the castle.

"So far so good!" Orufoo murmured.

Corranda's body trembled with anxiety as she and her two companions slipped through the black recesses of the castle shadows. She had never imagined there could be so many goblins in one place; the gruesome creatures seemed to ooze out of every nook and cranny. Fortunately, most were so drunk or engaged in other dreadful amusements that Corranda, Orufoo, and Shutakee managed to wind their way deeper and deeper into the core of the brooding fortress without being detected.

Shutakee finally brought them to a halt behind a dark stone pillar. "Look there across the courtyard," the crow whispered to her friends. "There's the statue of Odjin that Ukagee told us about."

Corranda looked upwards, but beheld the colossal sculpture of the witch for only a moment. Of more importance to her was finding the entrance to the dungeon.

"That must be it," she told her friends as she squinted through the night to spot a small opening set within the castle walls. The dark archway had no gate or door that she could see, but it was patrolled by a pair of heavily armed guards.

"We'll need to get past those two fiends," Shutakee said.

"Leave them to me," Orufoo declared.

The sly fox left the shadows of their hiding place and

trotted across the courtyard. Once he reached the dungeon door, he sat down on his haunches in plain view of the guards.

"What upsee here?" one of the guards cried. "Do you see this beasty, Byle? How he wander into middle of castle?"

Byle scratched his large, bumpy head in confusion. "Me don't know, Korn!" he said to his partner. "Maybe he losty lost!"

Korn and Byle clutched nervously at their weapons as Orufoo greeted them with a broad, mischievous grin. This smile soon turned into a snicker, and the next thing Korn and Byle knew, the fox was rolling about on the ground as if he was enjoying a great belly laugh at their expense.

"You ever see a beasty laugh before?" Korn asked.

"Nope," Byle replied. "Do you thinky he laughy at us? Look at me, Korny—maybe me have pimple on my forehead!"

"Your whole facey face covered in pimples!" Korn retorted. "He no laughy at just the one!"

Once Orufoo was sure he had the goblins' attention, he got up and moved a little farther away from the guards, laughing the whole time.

"Something sure hearty-har-har to that critter," Korn said angrily. He had never known an animal to possess the ability to laugh or smile, but here was an insolent fox, laughing at them all the same. He watched as Orufoo moved even farther away, still chuckling.

"Little beasty beast getting away," Byle pointed out.

"This ridiculous!" Korn declared, raising his sword. "C'mon! Let's go getty beast and eaty him!"

167

"Yeah!" Byle said indignantly. "We have a little midnighty snacky snack!"

Without another thought, Korn and Byle abandoned their post and chased Orufoo across the courtyard and into the night.

"I hope he's all right," Corranda fretted, still hiding in the shadows.

"He's smarter than those two, don't worry," Shutakee said. "Come on, Corra, let's go before those guards return!"

Accompanied now by only the crow, Corranda crept across the castle square and descended into the dungeons. The way was dark and poorly lit and Corranda stumbled more than once on the twisting stairwell that tunneled into the depths of the castle.

After some time, they reached the bottom of the stairs. The walls dripped with slime and the two friends nearly choked on the stale, moldy air. They passed by a row of dungeon cells, but all were empty. It looked as if no one had been there for a long time, and Corranda began to wonder if the place was not altogether deserted. She was just about to say as much to Shutakee when the crow spoke first.

"We've found him, Corra!" Shutakee murmured excitedly, peering around a corner in the passage. "Quiet now! There's one more guard yet!"

Corranda snuck a glance around the edge of the wall and saw the dark and dingy compartment where her uncle lay propped against the wall. The cell had no front other than a row of rusted iron bars, and Corranda could see that it was cold and bare, without so much as a chair or a mattress. Rollick looked so old and forlorn that Corranda

felt her heart would break at the sight of him. She turned
her eyes to the large, repulsive goblin that stood watch in
front of the cell. He was a big creature for a goblin, and
armed with a sharpened battle axe. Corranda could see the
key to her uncle's prison hanging on a peg in the wall, right
behind the guard.

"We're so close!" Corranda said, turning back to Shutakee.

"I will take care of this guard," Shutakee assured her.
"The rest is up to you!"

"Thank you," Corranda said to the bird, stroking her
long dark feathers.

"I will meet you outside the castle walls," Shutakee said
as she took to the air.

As soft as an autumn wind, the crow swooped down

from the shadows and attacked the unsuspecting goblin guard. Shutakee's beak was so hard and sharp that it seemed as if it had been forged from iron, and even the goblin's helmet did not protect him from her furious blows. Finally the hideous creature turned and fled, screaming and flailing as Shutakee chased him down the corridor.

The way was finally clear for Corranda and she rushed over to the prison cell. "Uncle Rollick!" she cried.

"Corra! Is that you?" Rollick exclaimed, rushing to the door of his prison. "What are you doing here?"

"I came for you," Corranda replied, clutching the old dwarf's hand between the bars. "I'm going to rescue you!"

"Corra, you shouldn't have come here!" Rollick warned. "You must leave, child, before it's too late!"

"I'm not going without you," Corranda told him.

"You don't understand, Corra," Rollick implored. "There are things I haven't told you!"

"Like what?" Corranda asked. "You're not making any sense, Uncle! What do you mean?"

Rollick meant to tell Corranda right there and then about the truth of her royal heritage, but before he could utter another word, a sinister heckle suddenly emanated from the dungeon shadows.

Rollick gasped. Corranda let her uncle's hand fall from her own and turned to face the darkness. She had never met Odjin, but somehow she knew that the ominous laughter belonged to the beautiful and evil sorceress.

Chapter 24

✵

Shutakee Falls

S hutakee chased the goblin guard through the maze of dungeon corridors and stairwells. She knew she needed to drive him as far away as possible from Corranda in order to help the girl escape with her uncle.

"Rotten birdy!" the goblin screamed as he raced down the castle passageways, desperately trying to avoid Shutakee's sharp beak. "Little birdy birdy gonna get what's coming to it!"

The vile beast suddenly ducked into a nearby doorway. Shutakee followed him, only to find herself right in the middle of a waiting pack of goblins!

The first goblin turned and smiled at Shutakee with a malicious, toothy grin. He had led her into a trap! "Friendy friends!" the goblin lisped. "Let's getty that awful birdy!"

The goblins instantly raised their rusty swords and broken spears and began slashing at Shutakee. With a squawk, Shutakee turned about and soared back down the passageway from where she had come, the entire goblin horde close on her tail.

I can't lead them back to Corra! Shutakee told herself. She zipped through the dark interior of the castle, taking every turn and door she could find, trying to evade the

goblins' weapons while at the same time leading them as far astray as possible. Then Shutakee suddenly saw a beam of moonlight shining through the musty darkness.

It's a window! Shutakee exclaimed to herself. If she could just make it to the open window, she could flee to the safety of the skies.

Without another thought, the feisty black crow soared towards the light. She was almost at the window when she suddenly felt the sickening crunch of a goblin's club against her wing. With a shriek of pain, Shutakee crumbled to the floor of the castle corridor in a shower of smashed and broken feathers. Freedom, which had seemed hers but for a fleeting moment, was now gone. Her wing lay bent and crippled at her side, flight impossible.

The goblins approached her, their large eyes glowing with their devious intent.

"That goody good shot, Gobb!" one of the goblins said, slapping the back of the gangly beast who had hit Shutakee with the club. "Now we feasty feast on little birdy!"

Shutakee cawed with warning at the encroaching goblins, but she knew she could not protect herself against so many. She looked desperately about her surroundings, but could find no escape. Then, out of the corner of her eye, she spied a small hole in the wall where a brick had dislodged and fallen away. There was no time to deliberate the plan; the wounded crow quickly scrambled across the floor and plunged through the crevice in the wall. The hole opened into a large, dark room. Shutakee could hear the goblins pounding furiously at the wall behind her, enraged by her escape. Shutakee's wing throbbed with pain, but she knew that she was out of danger. The goblins did not appear to know how to get to her, and as long as she could stay hidden, she would be safe.

In the blackness, Shutakee could not tell exactly what was in the room, but she did detect a great many crates and casks lining the walls. She picked her way across the floor and wedged herself in behind one of the many containers.

This must be a storeroom, Shutakee thought to herself. *Well, for now, it will have to store me!*

The injured crow closed her eyes and tried to forget about the flaring pain that coursed through her body. She knew that for her rescue would be out of the question, for none of her friends would know what had befallen her. Somehow she would have to survive long enough to find her own way out of the castle.

Chapter 25

✺

Rollick's Secret Revealed

Odjin sauntered out of the shadows and approached Rollick's cell, where Corranda stood frozen with fear.

"Indeed," the witch hissed as she cornered Corranda against the iron bars of Rollick's prison cell. "There are a great many things the old man neglected to tell you, my dear, sweet child."

"Leave her be, Odjin!" Rollick cried, hurling himself desperately against the bars.

"Silence, old fool!" Odjin commanded. She reached through the bars and with incredible physical strength, struck Rollick so hard that the weakened prisoner went reeling to the floor.

Corranda was speechless. Odjin's beauty, so cold and hard, was more powerful than anything she had ever imagined.

"Now," Odjin said as she pushed Corranda against the wall, "let's see if you are indeed who I think you are!" The witch yanked back the girl's hair and instantly found what she had been desperately in search of for fifteen long years: the tiny symbol of a crown upon Corranda's neck.

"It's true!" Odjin cackled. "You are the missing princess

of Kendar!"

Corranda stared at the witch in bewilderment. "Princess?" she cried. "What are you talking about!?"

"I'm so sorry, Corra," Rollick sobbed from behind his prison bars. "I meant to tell you! I should have told you!"

"No!" Corranda exclaimed, shaking her head in disbelief. "It's not true! It can't be true!"

"Of course it's true!" Odjin snapped. "You possess the unmistakable proof: the mark of the crown upon your neck!"

Corranda's eyes overflowed with tears as she remembered the story that Zolga, the old beggar woman, had told her so long ago about the lost princess of Kendar. Could she really be that princess? Corranda reached behind her neck, as if she might be able to actually feel the symbol of the crown. She could not, of course; she had lived her entire life without knowing she carried the enchanted mark. Although it all seemed so fantastical, somehow, deep inside, she knew the witch had spoken the truth.

"Uncle Rollick!" Corranda cried, looking across at the shaken dwarf. "Why didn't you tell me? I don't understand!"

"Your entire life has been a lie, it seems," Odjin gloated. "Perhaps we should punish the old man for his deception! What do you think, child?"

"Leave him be!" Corranda pleaded, clutching the witch's arm.

Odjin merely shrugged the girl away. Taking the key down from its peg on the wall, the witch opened the door to Rollick's cell and dragged him out into the corridor.

"Foolish old man," Odjin uttered. "You think you love the girl so much? Now you shall know the true power of love!"

The witch grabbed Rollick by the scruff of the neck and, lifting him completely off the ground, forced him to gaze upon her enchanting beauty.

Corranda watched in shock as her uncle began to transform right before very eyes. His short, stubby arms became thin and wiry, and his long beard receded until it was nothing more than a few scraggly hairs. In only a matter of seconds he had mutated into the wretched form of a goblin, and Odjin dropped him to the floor in a writhing heap.

"No longer shall you go by the name of Rollick," Odjin pronounced. "Forever more be known as Kolick!"

"Yes, yes, oh pretty mistress," Rollick submitted in his new, distorted body. "Kolick be good goblin. Kolick serve witchy well!"

"Oh, Uncle Rollick," Corranda sobbed. She held her arms out to the goblin who only moments before had been her beloved uncle, but the vicious creature only returned her affection by snapping at her with his long, crooked teeth. "I was so close to saving you!" Corranda murmured in despair.

"Close!" Odjin chortled. "What a silly girl you are! You were not even remotely close to rescuing him! Don't you see? Everything here has transpired according to my own plan! I knew you would come, my foolish child . . . I never intended to execute the dwarf; he was nothing more than bait, to lure you into my trap! And so I just waited for you to come, my dear princess. The minute you entered my valley, I knew of it! It was by my own command that my goblins left you alone, so that I might test your mettle. I wanted to see what type of rescue you might mount. And this was the best you could do? I'm disappointed to say the least. You are not even half the person your father was!"

Corranda had never known hatred, but now it welled within her, a dark, seething anger that she felt for the evil witch. In a sudden outburst of fury, Corranda threw herself at Odjin, railing her with blows from her fists.

Odjin was unfazed by Corranda's assault. Grabbing the girl by her long red hair, she led her away down the dungeon corridor with an evil smirk.

"Do not worry, my precious!" Odjin informed Corran-

177

da. "The old man's fate is nothing compared to that which will befall you!"

"And what is that?" Corranda asked.

"You shall see," Odjin responded, glaring down at the girl with unfettered delight. "The people of this wretched land have been nursing a hope for over fifteen years that you would one day return to save them; at last I shall crush their vexing spirit!"

"Haven't the people suffered enough?" Corranda asked as she wriggled within the witch's strong grasp.

"What do they know of suffering?" Odjin demanded angrily. "Do they know the pain of my heart? No! I will not stop until every one of them loves me."

"Then they will all be goblins," Corranda retorted.

"Then it will be so," the witch replied with an icy sneer.

Odjin's first action was to order Corranda's hair chopped short so that the mark upon her neck would be clearly visible and her identity indisputable. Corranda tried to keep a brave face as Captain Wort lopped off her long red tresses with his pair of notched, rusty scissors, but she could not prevent the tears from rolling down her cheeks. Odjin watched the haircut with amusement, standing before the girl's chair while Jurm and the rest of her goblin servants attended to her own long, flaxen ringlets with an array of golden combs and brushes.

"Gently, my dear malodorous mischief-makers," Odjin advised her goblins as she paused to regard herself in her mirror. "Beauty is precious and must be handled with utmost care and attention."

"Yes mistress, we make you look pretty pretty," Jurm assured the witch.

"Now look over at that miserable girl," Odjin declared with a wave of her hand in Corranda's direction. "Look at the soft curls that fall from her head. Have you ever seen such an ugly thing in all your life?"

"No one so ugly as girly girl!" Wort bellowed, the drool dribbling over his fleshy chin and onto Corranda's head as he finished the last of his snipping.

Odjin showed Corranda the mirror and the girl gasped at the sight of her shorn head. Her beautiful locks, which she had worn all her life, were now lying in a heap on the floor, and all she had left was a short, ragged head of hair.

"A style befitting a princess, to be sure!" Odjin mocked.

Once the mark upon Corranda's neck was plain for all to see, Odjin chained the girl in the middle of the castle square so that the people from the surrounding villages could come to witness the princess in all her humility.

"What about girly's little pipey pipe?" Captain Wort asked Odjin. "You want me takey it away or breaky it?"

"Leave it," Odjin replied in a dismissive tone. "Perhaps she shall play a sad song for the crowds, like a beggar in the street!" Odjin laughed out loud at the idea. "What do you think, my dear?" Odjin asked the enchained girl. "Do you have a melancholy melody you'd like to share with us?"

Corranda ignored the question.

"What, no music in your sad soul?" Odjin asked.

"Do with me as you will," Corranda finally murmured, staring forlornly at the ground. "I care not anymore."

"Oh, but you will," Odjin told the girl. "You see, you shall remain here now for seven days and nights."

"And then what?" Corranda asked.

"Then you will die," Odjin replied simply.

She turned her back and sauntered away to attend to her evening bath of perfumed soaps and fragrant oils, leaving Corranda to contemplate her fate in the middle of the castle square, beneath the cold and somber shadows of the witch's own commanding statue.

Chapter 26

ॐ

New Allies

Shutakee could not tell how much time had passed since she had first crawled into the dark storeroom after being wounded by the goblin's club. No one had disturbed her hiding place, but her wing still ached with pain, and she was hungry and thirsty. At first she thought she was in some sort of pantry, invoking a hope that she would easily find something to eat. But as the crow's eyes became accustomed to the darkness, she realized that she had hidden in one of Odjin's many coffers and there was nothing in the room other than caskets of gold, silver, and jewels. To Shutakee these treasures were worthless, for they would do nothing to sustain her, nor heal her wing.

The crow dozed, passing in and out of sleep, growing weaker and weaker with each hour that crept by. She supposed she would die in the cold, dark room, but she was helpless to do anything about it.

Then, a day after her injury, Shutakee suddenly awoke to find herself staring into the glowing yellow eyes of a large gray cat.

"Keep away!" Shutakee warned, though her throat was so dry and parched she could barely issue the threat. "I'll peck your eyes out yet!"

"Relax, my friend," the cat purred. "If I wanted to harm you, I would have done so already. Look, I have brought you some food."

Shutakee suddenly noticed a clump of water-soaked bread lying by her side and eagerly devoured it. The cat patiently waited for Shutakee to finish her meal before speaking again. "Food is scarce here," the gray feline said, "but I shall try to bring you more shortly."

"Why didn't you just eat me?" Shutakee asked suspiciously.

"I am not a hunter," the cat informed her. "My name is Pasha and I have lived in the castle my entire life, nearly sixteen years. Once I was the pet of Queen Anya of Kendar. There was a time when I was accustomed to eating from platters of gold and silver; of course, that was long ago, before the dark times. Now it is all I can do to scavenge a meal from scraps leftover by the witch's gluttonous goblins."

"I thank you, Pasha, for sharing your food," the crow said gratefully.

"Are you the one they call Shutakee?" Pasha asked.

"Yes!" the bird exclaimed with some surprise. "How do you know who I am?"

"You travel with Korr-an-rah," Pasha stated. "Stories of your adventures together proceed you. I first heard about you from Jumba the cow."

"Jumba!" Shutakee uttered. "She's alive then?"

"Yes, and lucky to be so," Pasha replied, as she lifted a hind leg to scratch the back of her ear. "If the old cow did not provide such delicious milk, I'm sure those loathsome goblins would have eaten her long ago. Now they keep her locked away in the stables where she toils to produce cream for Odjin's own breakfast. I visit her when I get the chance, for she tells amusing stories about your friends, the otter and the fox with the terrible sense of humor!"

"Yes," Shutakee murmured as she recalled her companions. "Orufoo and Kapoora! I have no idea what has become of them, let alone Corra!"

"I have heard from my friend, Ferajoo the bat, that the fox and the otter are safe, hiding out together on the other side of the river," Pasha said. "As for your human friend—what did you call her—Corra? She has been captured by Odjin and now sits in chains in the middle of the castle square."

"Captured!" Shutakee gasped. "Why? What does Odjin

184

intend to do with her?"

"To kill her, I'm afraid," Pasha explained. "You see, Korr-an-rah is not only special to us, mere animals and birds like ourselves, Shutakee."

"What do you mean?" the crow asked.

"She may be Corra or Korr-an-rah, but she is also Corranda, rightful heir to the throne of Kendar and queen of the humans!" Pasha divulged. "The land is buzzing with the news that she has been revealed!"

"Well, I haven't gotten much news down here," Shutakee admitted as she tried to absorb what the cat had told her.

"You never knew about her, who she really was?" Pasha asked.

"She didn't know herself," Shutakee responded. "I suppose I shouldn't be surprised. Corra is a unique human. Have you talked to her, Pasha?"

"No," the cat replied. "She is heavily guarded. I am old and slow now. It might not take much for those goblins to impale me with one of their spears if I go out into the openness of the castle square!"

"You have to try!" Shutakee urged. "Somehow we must try and save her! I wish my wing were better!"

"How bad is it?" Pasha asked the crow.

"It's not as bad as I first thought," Shutakee said, moving the wing slightly to demonstrate its condition. "Still, I won't be able to fly for a few days. How long does Corra have?"

"There are only six days left until the execution," Pasha said. "Still, I don't know what we can do to help her."

"Corra has powers of her own," Shutakee told the cat. "Now is the time for her to realize them!"

"Her spirit is broken," Pasha confided. "I doubt she can muster much hope."

"You must help her regain it," Shutakee implored. "It's up to you now!"

Pasha sat back on her haunches and closed her eyes in deep thought. "I will do as you say," the feline said finally with a decided determination. "I will go tell her of her mother and father and of her great heritage. After all, I did not slink about this dank dungeon for fifteen years only to abandon the daughter of my mistress in her most dire hour!"

"Tell Corra I will come to her as soon as I am able," Shutakee said.

"I will," Pasha promised as she rose to all fours and turned to go. "I will send word to your friends, Orufoo and Kapoora, about what has happened to you and in the morning I will bring you some more food."

"Thank you, Pasha," Shutakee said. "You are very brave."

Upon leaving Shutakee, Pasha went to find her friend, Ferajoo the long-eared bat. Pasha moved with slowness and age, but she knew the castle like the back of her paw and was able to travel its network of tunnels and halls without being spotted by Odjin's goblins.

Ferajoo was sleeping in his usual spot, a high crook in the ceiling, when Pasha came to see him. He had two big pointed ears and a small furry brown body which was hidden from view by a pair of long leathery wings that were wrapped around him in a protective shell while he slept.

"Ferajoo!" the cat meowed. "Wake up! It's me, Pasha!"

The bat opened one sleepy eye. "It's not time for hunting yet," the nocturnal creature squeaked, and promptly shut his eye again.

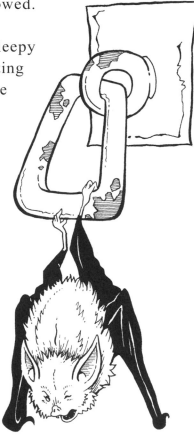

"This is more important than hunting," Pasha told him. "Wake up!"

"Oh, very well then," Ferajoo muttered. He stretched out his long thin wings and fluttered down alongside the cat. "I see those goblins haven't managed to get their claws into you yet," Ferajoo joked. "Then again, you might be too old and tough for them to bother with you!"

"Worry for yourself," Pasha said. "A goblin would eat you just as soon as anything else."

"True enough," Ferajoo responded with a wide yawn that revealed his tiny sharp teeth. "What's so important that you have to wake me up so early?"

"I'm going to talk to Corranda," Pasha said.

"That's dangerous," Ferajoo warned. "She's surrounded by goblin guards. Why do you want to do that?"

187

"She needs me," Pasha said. "She's all alone."

"Maybe I should go instead," Ferajoo suggested. "If those goblins get frisky, I'll just fly away."

"No, I need you to do something else," Pasha said.

"What's that?" Ferajoo asked curiously.

"You must spread word across the land about Corranda," Pasha said. "Everyone must know! Go tell Orufoo and Kapoora to prepare themselves, for I think something is about to happen. We must all be ready."

"I don't understand," Ferajoo said. "Ready for what?"

"I'm not sure," Pasha confessed. "I just have a feeling in these old feline bones of mine. So go, Ferajoo, go tell them all to be ready. Go tell Lubakai the wolf and Ajapaska the rabbit. Go to Ukagee the sturgeon and Jamakee the gull. Tell Ixximo, queen of the honey bees, and Manchipukoo, the great bear of the north. Tell them all, Ferajoo!"

"I will do as you say," the bat declared. "Though part of me thinks you are crazy! Still, if it will help Corranda, then I will fly to the ends of the earth!"

With that, the small furry bat took to the air and disappeared through the nearest window into the fading light of late afternoon. Pasha watched him go, then turned to make her way towards Corranda, the lost princess of Kendar.

Chapter 27

❧

Pasha's Tale

Sitting chained and humbled in the castle square, Corranda felt truly alone for the first time in her life. Her friends were nowhere to be found, not even Shutakee, who the girl thought might circle overhead to offer her comfort. Her shackles chafed her wrists, and she was given little to eat or drink. Escape was hopeless, for she was under the watch of a dozen goblin guards who relieved the boredom of their duties by poking and prodding her with sticks and spears. Worst of all, Corranda could not rid herself of the image of her Uncle Rollick transforming into a goblin. Once so kind and gentle, the dwarf was now one of the most gruesome creatures alive, and it was all due to Odjin's evil beauty.

Corranda shuddered whenever she thought of the witch. Odjin was more powerful than she had ever imagined. The witch had destroyed the entire land with her beauty, and now she would destroy Corranda too. Alas, the girl's spirit withered and weakened to the point that she had no hope at all.

Then, on the second afternoon of her imprisonment, Corranda noticed an old, grizzled cat hiding in the stony crook of a nearby wall. The cat was so still and patient that

189

at first Corranda thought her eyes must be playing a trick on her. The cat was definitely there, however, and for the entire evening it watched the princess with its large yellow eyes. Corranda was tempted to call out to the cat, or play a song for it on her pipe, but she knew any such attention would cause the goblins to notice the animal and harm it. Instead, Corranda contented herself with watching the old gray cat out of the corner of her eye, curious to see what the creature would do.

Finally, as darkness descended and Corranda's guards distracted themselves by gorging on food and wine, the cat crept down the wall and came before the girl in the pale light of the moon.

"Why do you come here?" Corranda whispered to the feline. "These goblins are savage and ruthless and will hurt you if given the chance."

"It's a risk I must take," the cat replied. "My name is Pasha and I have come to bring you news, Corranda."

"Why do you call me this?" the Princess asked. "Most animals know me as Korr-an-rah."

"The names are alike," the cat remarked. "Still, I knew you first as Corranda. It is what I've always called you, and it is what I will call you yet."

"I don't understand," Corranda said.

"I get ahead of myself," Pasha declared. "I will explain, but first I must tell you about your friends."

"What has become of them?" Corranda asked, fidgeting uncomfortably in her chains.

"I have received word that Orufoo and Kapoora are hiding in the woods on the other side of the river," Pasha replied. "They are afraid for you, princess, but they are safe. As for Shutakee, her wing was damaged in a scuffle with Odjin's goblins."

"Is she all right?" Corranda gasped.

"Yes, she is recovering well enough," Pasha said. "I spoke with her myself this afternoon. Her wing will heal in time, but I doubt she will be strong enough to visit you for another three or four days."

"Everything has turned out poorly," Corranda murmured. "It's my fault that Shutakee is wounded—she risked herself to help me."

Just then one of the goblin guards looked up from his dinner and Pasha quickly ducked beneath the girl's dress.

"Who girly talky to?" the goblin demanded.

"Just to myself," Corranda retorted. "It's a much better pastime than listening to you fill your gullet!"

"You crazy girly girl," the goblin lisped. "You keepy it down. Some us wanty get some snoozy in!"

Corranda glared as the ugly creature turned his back on her to finish his meal.

"This is dangerous," Pasha mewed as she poked her head out from beneath Corranda's dress. "We'll have to be more careful!"

"Maybe you should go," Corranda suggested.

"No, what I have to tell you is too important," Pasha said. "Come curl up on the floor, Corranda and I will nestle within your arms so that the guards won't see me."

Corranda did as the cat instructed and Pasha was soon snuggled next to her chest. The cat was warm and Corranda could feel her soft purring against her skin.

"What's so dangerous that you must risk your life to tell me?" Corranda asked once the cat was settled.

"It's about yourself," Pasha said. "I must tell you who you are!"

"You're too late for that," Corranda muttered. "I already know that. Odjin told me."

"You may know it, but I don't think you understand it," Pasha claimed. "You see, my years are long now, so long that I can remember the kingdom in happier days, before Odjin became queen. Even your own mother stroked my fur as a kitten!"

"You knew my mother!?" Corranda exclaimed.

"Yes, for I have lived in the castle all my life," Pasha

told her. "I was once your mother's pet and went everywhere with her. I remember the night you were born, Corranda, for I was there."

"I have no recollection of my mother," Corranda said sadly.

"She was a great woman," Pasha said. "I loved her very much. But the tale I wish to tell you occurred before my time. It was passed down to me by my own grandmother, who herself was just a kitten when Queen Anya came to Kendar."

"Anya was my mother's name?" Corranda asked. "What do you mean, she came to Kendar?"

"So many questions!" Pasha mewed. "Patience, princess, and I will endeavor to answer them all for you! You should know, Corranda, that your mother was not of Kendar, but from an enchanted island country far beyond the distant horizon. She was a young woman when she came, and not without magic herself."

"She was a sorceress?" Corranda asked.

"Not in so many words," Pasha said. "She had an affinity with nature and could understand the language of animals, much like yourself. All the people of Kendar were amazed by her, but none more than your father, King Daron. He fell in love with young Anya, and she with him. But she was not the only one to long for Daron's heart. There was another, a young apprentice of magic, who pined for your father. She competed to become Daron's queen, but your father's love for Anya was too strong. And the young apprentice turned wicked and spiteful with jealousy, for she could not cope with this rejection. She vowed never to lose the love of another and locked herself away to master her dark powers."

"Odjin," Corranda whispered. "It was Odjin."

"Yes," Pasha purred. "She is old now, though you would never know it to gaze upon her beauty. Her black magic gives her the appearance of youth, but inside she is old and vile."

"And my mother and father?" Corranda prompted.

"They were married," Pasha continued. "And the land was joyful. But shortly after the wedding, Anya was visited by a horrible nightmare, in which the land was laid to waste and all the people enslaved. She knew she could not ignore the warning of this dream, so she let her heart guide her through the country until she came to a quiet grove in the far northern reaches of the kingdom. And here she planted a seed that was native to her own country, a magical seed from which sprouted forth a magical tree. And the tree grew quickly, through the day and night, becoming in years what most trees become only in centuries. This is your enchanted tree, Corranda, the tree which gave you both your pipe and your power."

"This is an amazing tale," Corranda said, stroking Pasha's soft gray fur. "But what am I to do with this legacy? How should I use this power?"

"That is an answer I do not know," Pasha admitted. "But it has a purpose; this you must understand. Don't you see, Corranda? This is why I told you this tale, so that you might know that there are forces other than evil at work in the world."

"I am grateful to you," Corranda told the cat. "I feel

helpless still, but grateful nonetheless."

"I must go now, princess," Pasha said, rising and touching Corranda on the cheek with her pink nose. "I will come and see you again, but now I must check on Shutakee."

Corranda nodded, but barely heard the cat's words, for her mind was clouded with thoughts of her mother and father. Pasha slunk into the darkness, leaving Corranda to close her eyes and dream of the parents she had never known.

The days following passed quickly for the enslaved

princess. Each morning brought a new crowd of onlookers
who came streaming into the castle to see if Odjin's boasts
about capturing the long-lost princess were true. They
didn't need to look beyond the mark upon Corranda's neck.
This was the proof that the witch had not lied, and when the
people saw the symbol of the crown, they wept and moaned
with despair. The story of the hidden Princess had represented their last nugget of hope, and now that too had been
destroyed.

Corranda's own heart swelled with sorrow and even
though Pasha came to sit with her through the darkest hours
of the night, the girl could not be comforted. She felt she
had failed everyone.

Then, on the final night before her scheduled execution,

Shutakee fluttered into the castle square, her wing finally strong enough to fly. The goblin guards drank and threw dice at their posts, unaware of the crow's presence.

"Corra!" Shutakee whispered. "I have come to you finally! How are you?"

"How should I be?" Corranda retorted. "Tomorrow will be my end!"

"Then why do you sit here weeping and feeling sorry for yourself?" Shutakee cried. "How will this save you? Where is my friend who would stand up and fight for herself?"

"That is not I," Corranda told the crow. "Perhaps you are thinking of my mother."

"And what about your mother?" Shutakee demanded. "Have you not heard old Pasha's tale? Your mother planted the tree for you! It was she who gave you your magic so that you might defy Odjin and liberate the land!"

"But I never knew my mother," Corranda persisted. "What did she mean me to do with this power? I don't understand . . . is there no help you can give me?"

"What can I give you that you do not already possess?" Shutakee asked. "Who knows better than the animals and birds the cold unfairness of the earth? When I fly over the fields, goblins and humans alike throw stones at me to break my wings. And when Orufoo drinks from the river, the villagers chase after him with sticks and clubs. And they hunt Kapoora with spears and nets so that they might skin her and wear her as a hat! We are mere animals, and all the world seeks to destroy us with its cruelty and anger. Yet you were kind and happy, Korr-an-rah! This I know: the first

197

time I heard the music emanating from your pipe, I knew your heart burst with a power so good and pure that no witch, no evil, was strong enough to match it! You ask for help, but listen to me, child! You can only help yourself."

Corranda stared at the crow, wiping the tears from her eyes. For the first time in seven days, her thoughts turned from self-pity to dwell on her friends. She thought of all the injustices that plagued the kingdom, the kingdom which was meant for her to guard and protect.

Finally she said, "I understand now. I know what I must do."

Chapter 28

❧

Corranda of Kendar

T he day of Corranda's scheduled execution was dark and dreary. The light of the autumn sun was blurred by a veil of pale clouds that infused the air with a cold chill, while the tattered banners atop the castle spires wavered solemnly in the wind.

It was a somber mood that reflected the very spirit of Kendar's people. Today the life of their princess was to be extinguished, and with her, their final flicker of hope. People had no desire to witness Corranda's execution, but this was Odjin's moment of triumph, and she was not about to have it spoiled. She ordered her goblins to round up the people from the nearby villages and farms and by noon the castle square was packed with reluctant spectators.

As part of her ploy to increase the drama of the day, Odjin had removed Corranda from the square earlier in the morning, and the princess now awaited her fate deep in the dungeons of the castle keep. Confined to the darkness of a dingy prison cell, Corranda drifted in and out of sleep, dreaming of happier times when she lived with her uncle in their humble cottage in the woods. To the girl who now wrestled with the fact that she was heir to an entire kingdom, those days seemed so very far away.

At midday, Corranda was awakened by a sharp jab from Captain Wort's notched and soiled sword.

"Wakey, wakey!," the goblin commanded with a malicious grin that exposed his slimy yellow teeth. "Do you knowy what day it is?"

"My day of truth?" Corranda retorted with a hard glare.

"Truthy truth is that you gonna get it," Wort sneered, making an ominous slicing gesture across his throat with a long bony finger.

Then, with a loud laugh, the repugnant creature yanked Corranda to her feet and brought her before Odjin.

"My dear, disheveled child," the witch murmured, overlooking the girl with a critical eye. "What an ugly, pitiful little thing you have become! You really don't amount to much, Princess Corranda, do you?"

Corranda refused to react to the witch's taunt and Odjin afforded herself a haughty laugh. "Stoic in the end, I suppose," she said. "Well, come child, your people await you!"

Followed by her entourage of goblin servants, Odjin led the enchained Princess Corranda into the castle square and onto a low podium in the middle of the crowd. The moment was strangely quiet, the tears and wails of the people silenced by the appearance of the tall, imposing witch and her ill-fated prisoner.

"Here is your beloved princess, upon whom you have rested all of your hopes," the witch proclaimed, her voice breaking loud and clear across the square. "And see, the girl shall die by my own doing! So pay reverence to me, my subjects, for no one is more powerful than I!"

"No!" Corranda cried suddenly, stepping forward. "You

are not so powerful, Odjin! I, as the true and rightful leader of Kendar, defy you!"

A gasp of astonishment rippled through the crowd, but Odjin did not flinch. She turned to confront Corranda with a cool glare, then let out a loud, sinister laugh. "What an amusing girl you are," she mocked. "Defy me? By what means? How do you expect to overthrow me, my dear—with your little pipe?"

This, of course, was exactly what Corranda intended to do and, before the witch could react, the princess put the pipe to her lips and played a song so loud and vibrant that it seemed to travel throughout the entire kingdom.

At first Odjin thought that Corranda had lost her mind, to play her pipe and think that it had the power to save her. Then the witch heard a distant sound replying to Corranda's song. The noise started out quietly, then began to intensify, growing closer and clearer, louder and stronger. The earth rumbled, the river gurgled and the air itself seemed to tremble with anticipation until suddenly an enormous army of animals, as numberless as the stars in the sky, converged upon the castle in a full-scale invasion!

The attack seemed to come from every direction. It came from the skies where Shutakee swooped down amidst a giant flock of birds. It came from the river where Kapoora headed a frightening assault on the castle walls with an entire swarm of water dwellers at her side. And it came from the ground, where Orufoo charged through the gates of the citadel with a huge herd of land beasts stampeding behind him. Here was Ferajoo the long-eared bat, Pasha the old gray feline, and Jumba the cow, busted free of her stable. Here too were the friends Corranda had met along her journey: Queen Ixximo and her hive of honey bees, Manchipukoo the giant bear, the beavers Eyako and Wakashai, and Ukagee the mighty sturgeon king. The call had been heard by creatures from all across Kendar: Chukolo the owl, Rubukoo the stag, Urjeepa the wren, Jamakee the gull, Ajapaska the rabbit, Torrodo the bull frog, Kalyxxa the dragonfly, and Lubakai the wolf. There were others too, the likes of which Corranda had never seen, for Ferajoo's call had echoed through the land like an unstoppable force, down the Uka River and out to the vast Samboora Sea, across the flowering Penelopee Plains and up the towering Mountains of the Seven Winds, through the arid deserts of Jakkar, and deep into the lush jungles of Zamfu. Here were Rombolo the rhinoceros, Keramodee the great striped tiger, Pontolo the sand viper, Jaramundee the buffalo bull, Gondora the okapi, Subatai the swordfish, Nookachee the chamois, Chuwalla the road-runner, Porgerra the octopus, and Graffikee the gigantic golden eagle. Still there were more: antelope, swallows, and snapping green turtles; hawks, codfish, and spotted genets; sea lions, squirrels, and fan-tailed peacocks; lobsters, geese, and hoary-tusked boars. They had all assembled to hear the beckon of Corranda's pipe and now they descended upon Odjin's hapless goblin horde in a climactic, magical outburst of nature, hissing, growling, roaring, and squawking.

The first reaction of the people gathered in the square was to take cover from the animal charge, but when they realized that the creatures were attacking only the goblins, the citizens of Kendar found their courage. Some of them were armed with shovels and pitchforks, and with a rallying cry, they joined the animals in the assault on the witch's minions. The castle was soon engulfed in battle.

Odjin watched in angry desperation as the menagerie of creatures and humans overwhelmed her goblin throng.

"Cowards!" the witch screamed at her soldiers. "Stand up and fight, you filthy, flatulent, phlegm-flowing fiends! Look upon me! Know my beauty and obey!"

There was no command, however, that she could issue that would turn the hearts of her troops, for they were so scratched, pecked, clawed, and bitten that their only desire was for escape. For the first time in her reign, the witch's

beauty proved impotent and helpless.

Corranda lowered her pipe and stood proudly before the witch. "I am the one they call Korr-an-rah," she proclaimed over the deafening din of the battle. "Behold the crown upon my neck, witness the power of my song, and know, Odjin, that I am your Queen, Corranda of Kendar."

Odjin gulped as she suddenly realized Corranda's power; the girl commanded the greatest army in the world through the power of her pipe. Her heart beating with fear and anxiety, the witch turned and fled through the chaos, abandoning her goblins to the mercy of the animal throng.

Corranda had no intention of letting the witch escape. She leaped from the podium in pursuit of her foe, but fell to the ground beneath the weight of her chains.

"Corra, let me help you!" Kapoora cried, coming before the princess amidst the chaos of the battle.

"I need to get these shackles off!" Corranda exclaimed in desperation. "Odjin mustn't get away!"

"Patience, child!" Kapoora said, producing a ring of keys which she had ripped from the belt of one of the goblin guards. Using her dexterous paws, the otter quickly unlocked Corranda's cuffs and set her free. "Careful now!" Kapoora warned, but Princess Corranda had already dashed across the castle square, following the witch's trail.

Odjin made no hesitation in deciding her escape route. It was her intention to flee through the same secret passage that Rollick had used so many years ago to escape, but even before the witch reached the bottom of the stairs she found her way blocked by her greatest enemy—Corranda herself.

"I see now that your beauty is nothing more than a mask for your cowardice," Corranda uttered.

"You!" Odjin shrieked. "How did you know of this tunnel?"

"A little gray cat told me!" Corranda declared, standing boldly before the witch.

The mention of an animal caused Odjin to look over her shoulder in fright, but she quickly realized that Corranda was alone and without the protection of her companions. A fresh hope for victory sparked instantly within the crafty witch and she regained her composure.

"It is unfortunate, you know, that we are enemies," Odjin whispered as she cautiously approached Corranda.

"What do you mean?" Corranda demanded.

"Are we not the two mightiest people in the entire land?" Odjin asked, drawing closer to the princess in the darkness. "If we were to combine our powers, we would be invincible."

"I am not interested in the domination of the world," Corranda retorted. She instinctively stepped away from the witch, but found herself backed against the stony wall of the dungeon stairwell.

"But think, child!" Odjin cried, grasping Corranda by the shoulder with her smooth, long-fingered hand. "The rewards would be unimaginable! You could have anything you want!"

"I have everything I want!" Corranda declared.

"Do you?" the beautiful

sorceress asked, staring deeply into Corranda's eyes. "Do you really? When I look into your soul I see a sadness there. I see a child who never knew her own mother."

Corranda pulled back, startled at the witch's ability to read her one true sorrow. She tried to turn her eyes away from Odjin, but felt consumed by her radiance.

"We can change all that, you know," the sorceress said, affectionately stroking the girl's chin. "I have the power to give you a mother, Corranda."

"How can you do that?" Corranda exclaimed.

"With my magic," Odjin replied, and she seemed now to Corranda more beautiful and enchanting than ever. "I will be your mother, and you will be my daughter. I will love you all my days and it will be as if we had never been apart."

"N-n-no!" Corranda stammered. "I want my real mother . . . not you."

"Love me, child," Odjin implored, her power now overtaking the girl. "Love me and you will have a mother."

Corranda struggled to find a reason to resist Odjin's offer, but she was so enchanted by the witch's soft voice and seductive beauty that she could not form a single clear thought. In the passing of those few brief moments, Corranda's mind exploded with a thousand pictures of happiness and mirth as she imagined a life with her new mother—the most beautiful mother in the world. And yet, while Corranda's heart abounded with that fleeting, hollow joy, her outside began to suddenly alter into something hideous; her arms grew long and spindly, her skin turned gray and thick, and her nose and ears began to sprout long, course hair!

Then something deep inside the princess suddenly sprang to life and fought back against the witch's charm: it was the memory of her uncle. As she found the truth of Rollick's love and nurturing tucked deep within her heart, Corranda realized the falsity of Odjin's promises.

"Never!" Corranda cried as the spell melted away and her figure returned to its natural state. "I'll never join you!"

Still, while Odjin had failed in transforming Corranda into one of her wretched goblins, she had succeeded in distracting her. Even as the princess pulled back, the snarling sorceress reached out and ripped the magic pipe from Corranda's neck!

"You insolent girl!" the witch jeered. "Why would I share the world, when I could have it for myself?"

Odjin turned and dashed up the stairway with the pipe, climbing to the top of the castle walls, where she could look down upon the valley.

"Hear me!" the crazed sorceress screamed down to the earth. "Now I shall control the land, the sea, and even the sky!"

Corranda scrambled up the castle tower to stop the witch, but already she was too late. Odjin took up the pipe and began to play her own violent, tyrannical song.

But the magic was not to be for the vengeful sorceress. Music comes from the soul, and even though Odjin was beautiful and glamorous on the outside, inside she was as black and vile as the deepest dungeon. Corranda's songs were filled with joy and kindness, but when Odjin played the pipe, her music was fraught with anger and domination.

211

It was Odjin's will to control all the creatures of the world with the power of the pipe, but when they heard her ugly, malevolent song, they revolted. Instead of submitting to her desire, the animals turned on her, attacking her in even greater force than they had mustered against the goblin army. Every beast left its burrow to fight her, every insect seethed from the soil, and the earth quaked beneath the pounding of each paw and hoof. The river choked on a tidal wave of fish, and the sun was blotted out by the wings of birds.

Only too late did Odjin understand the terrible fate she had called upon herself. As the creatures of the world smashed against the tower, the floor crumbled beneath Odjin's feet and with a final shriek of anger, the witch plummeted to her doom. Corranda too fell amongst the toppling stones, and at first she thought she had met her end. Then at the last moment, Graffikee the giant eagle swooped down and took the girl up in his mighty claws. The last thing Corranda remembered before fainting was the enormous eagle placing her gently on the ground.

Chapter 29

෨෯

Return of the Crown

When Corranda awoke, it was to the soft lap of Orufoo's wet tongue against her face. She opened her eyes to see the fox standing over her with Kapoora and Shutakee by his side. Corranda slowly pulled herself up to gaze upon the remains of the battle. Graffikee had set her safely on the riverbank, but she was close enough to the island to see that nothing remained of the once mighty castle but a gigantic mound of blackened stones. The towers and turrets—even Odjin's colossal statue—had all crumbled to the ground. The valley was now quiet and solemn; the giant animal army Corranda had summoned with her pipe seemed to vanish into thin air.

"Where did everyone go?" the girl murmured, rubbing her aching head.

"Back to their homes," Shutakee said. "They've returned to the mountains, the jungles, and the ocean."

"But I don't understand," Corranda said. "How did they come here so quickly, from so far?"

"The magic of the pipe was greater than even we knew," Kapoora replied. "Ferajoo the bat spread word to all the creatures of the land to be ready for something great, but I don't think anything could have prepared them for the power

213

of your music. When they heard your song calling them to rise up against the goblins, their desire was so strong that for one magical moment, time and space had no meaning!"

Corranda reached instinctively to her chest to touch the pipe, but when it wasn't there, she remembered that Odjin had stolen it. "My pipe!" Corranda cried. "What has become of it? How am I able to talk to you without its power?"

"The pipe was lost when Odjin was destroyed," Orufoo told her. "But the magic was strong, Corra, and so connected to you that it lasts a little while yet."

"For how long?" the girl persisted.

"I'm afraid the magic is fading, even as we speak," Kapoora said gravely. "You will soon lose your ability to speak our language, Corra, and we cannot stay with you."

"Why?" Corranda exclaimed. "You can't just leave!"

"Corra, you are now queen of the land," Shutakee explained. "Perhaps it's better this way. No living thing can rule humans and animals both. You must take your place before your people."

"But you are my best friends!" Corranda said. "Stay with me! It doesn't matter to me if I can't speak your words!"

"Sweet child," Kapoora murmured, touching her nose to Corranda's cheek. "We are wild like the earth. We can no more live in a palace or castle than you can live in the sea. We must return to the river and the forest and the clouds and behave as wild creatures were meant to exist."

"We not forget you," Orufoo assured the girl, his words already becoming difficult for Corranda to understand. "I hope you not forget us, either. Rule kingdom wisely, Queen Korr-an-rah!"

With that, Orufoo, Kapoora, and Shutakee turned and disappeared into the woods, leaving Corranda to weep by herself near the remnants of the battle. She could not help feeling sorry for herself; she had defeated Odjin and released the land from the witch's iron rule, but in the process she had paid a great price.

How long she sat there, Corranda did not know, but after a time she noticed a small, stout figure approaching her across the withered grass. At first she thought it might be a goblin, but then she realized there was something strangely familiar about the figure.

"Uncle Rollick!" Corranda cried as she recognized the grizzled old man.

"Corra, I have found you!" the dwarf exclaimed, rushing forward to embrace her.

"You've changed into your old self again!" Corranda cried excitedly, leaning down to kiss her uncle on his round, bald head.

"Yes, my sweet child," Rollick said with a tear in his eye. "Odjin's demise has returned all the goblins to human form."

"Then Finn and Kess will get their parents back," Corranda murmured happily, "and Zolga will find her son!"

"Who are these people?" Rollick asked.

"Just friends I've met along the way," Corranda told the old man.

"I think I may have found another old companion of yours," Rollick said to the girl, pointing over his shoulder. "This strange animal won't stop following me!"

"Pasha!" Corranda exclaimed, looking up to see the old gray cat trailing behind Rollick. She picked up the feline and stroked her soft fur. Pasha purred in response to the

girl's warm hands, but Corranda could not understand the cat's speech. "The pipe was lost in the battle," Corranda told her uncle sadly.

"It's all right," Rollick consoled her. "Perhaps it has served its purpose."

"Poor old Pasha," Corranda murmured, turning her attention back to the cat. "I might not understand your words, but I love you just the same. You'll never have to forage the floor for food again!"

Rollick took Corranda's hand and as they left the riverbank, a sheet of clouds rolled into the sky and began to rain upon the thirsty land.

"Look, Corra!" Rollick said as the cool rain trickled over his wrinkled brow. "Maybe the drought is over!"

"The land will live again," the girl said.

Corranda was right. Slowly, fertility and prosperity returned to Kendar. The spring following the great battle, the banks of the Uka River swelled with life once again and the dry gray soil sprouted with new green grass. The trees bloomed with fruit, the fields teemed with crops, and the forests and meadows resonated with the joyful songs of wrens and thrushes. Houses were repaired, villages rebuilt, and eventually even the remnants of the old castle were cleared away, and a new one raised in its place.

After shedding their goblin forms, Rollick and Belarus were reunited and together they stood by Corranda as she assumed her rightful position on the throne of Kendar. She had lots to learn about leading a country, but with Rollick and Belarus to assist her, she came to rule Kendar wisely and kindly, as was her nature.

Through the years, the legend of Corranda grew in the minds of the people, and parents would tell their children stories of how their queen had once summoned the greatest army on earth, an army of animals. But despite the fact that she had lost the power to speak to the creatures of the land, Corranda never forgot her friends, and she knew that they had not forgotten her. For when Corranda passed by the river, the otters would raise their heads to chatter at her, and the crows would call to her from their perches in the trees, and sometimes, when she was really lucky, she would even catch a glimpse of a peculiar fox poking his head through the bushes to greet her with a long, friendly smile.